Women Speak
Volume Six

Edited by Kari Gunter-Seymour

Spoken Word and Fine Art Selections

WOMEN OF APPALACHIA PROJECT™

ISBN: 978-1-7354002-2-8
Sheila-Na-Gig Editions
Russell, KY

EDITOR: Kari Gunter-Seymour
LINE EDITOR: Kristine Williams
COVER DESIGN: Kari Gunter-Seymour
COVER ART: *Beautiful Misfits,* Diana Ferguson

INQUIRIES:
Kari Gunter-Seymour, Executive Director
womenofappalachia@gmail.com
www.womenofappalachia.com
FACEBOOK: Women of Appalachia Project

ACKNOWLEDGMENTS

A Place So Deep Inside America It Can't Be Seen (Sheila-Na-Gig Editions): "Pack Horse Librarians"
Appalachian Review: "Fish Fry"
Artemis Journal: "Contrary"
Black Mermaid (Argus House Press): "What Women Do," "The Woman is Round," "To the Woman I Saw Today Who Wept in Her Car"
Crimson Sunshine: "Birchie"
The Distance Between Blues (Finishing Line Press): "Stella's Dishes"
The Galway Review: "Black Pudding"
HeartWood Literary Magazine: "Lines of Disappearance, Chillicothe, Ohio, 2014-2015"
Infection House: "Wash Your Hands Child"
Imagine a Town (Sheila-Na-Gig Editions): "I'm from a one-way bus ticket"
JuxtaProse Literary Magazine: "Spitting Downstairs"
Lexington Poetry Month: "Exodus," "Radiation Therapy: A Baptism," "Reading the Obits"
Literary Accents: A Literary Journal: "The February Morning After We Fight," "Heritage"
The Mockingbird: "Heartpine," "Red Oak"
New Limestone Review: "Some Nights We Have the Moon"
Northern Appalachian Review: "Perfect Pitch"
Original Ruse (Accents Publishing): "Over-Easy at the All-Night Diner"
Pine Mountain Sand & Gravel: "Interview"
Pudding Magazine: The Journal of Applied Poetry: "Sanctuaries"
Rattle: "When Peeled Back"
South Dakota Review: "Hope Against Hope"
The Sow's Ear Poetry Review: "Counting Daddy Home"
Tin House Online: "Genealogical Trip to Pulaski, Virginia"
Unscathed (NightBallet Press): "Landscapes of Grief," "The Rib of Eve"
What Rough Beast (Indolent Books): "Trigger"

Contents

FINE ART

CONTRIBUTOR BIOS:

INTRODUCTION

Today, and for well over a century, Appalachians have been marginalized and stereotyped. This deliberate ploy has affected multiple generations and was intended to dehumanize and belittle so that major U.S. coal companies could gain access to Appalachia's immense coal reserves. It was at that time Appalachians began to be characterized as barefoot, overfed, under-educated and under-groomed, and the land was consumed by coal removal. When we Appalachians are portrayed as white trash, it is easier to pull off the ruse that coal companies were/are in the business to save Appalachia, rather than plunder.

With the collapse of the coal industry in the late 1950's, as mountain top mining was replaced by oil and natural gas, Appalachia became a junkyard. There was no way for previously hard-working miners to return to farming, as much of horticulture had been forsaken and strip mining had wrecked most of the land, leaving unemployment, lack of basic infrastructure, and no reasonable access to education. In addition to the coal industry, timber and iron industries further exploited the land and us, its native people.

After years of extreme living conditions–no electricity, running water, or proper sewage–in 1964, President Lyndon B. Johnson declared a "War on Poverty" focused on Appalachia. Federal money was legislated to create social welfare programs but no job or education programs, which served only to protect Appalachians from starvation, but deprived us of self-respect and hope. Women, more often than not, fell into greater poverty and ill health due to the death of partners and extremely inadequate medical care and nutrition during childbearing years.

Over the past 50+ years, further programs have been implemented, including those resulting in educational and training opportunities for Appalachians, though they are certainly not as robust as the national average. The economy of the region, once so dependent on mining, forestry, agriculture, and chemical industries, has gradually become more diversified. In spite of many generations of struggle and unfair policies, Appalachia is producing bright, talented individuals who are skilled, well educated, and very proudly tied to their Appalachian roots.

The "Women Speak" anthology series is an examination of the long-lasting effects of stereotypes and false narratives surrounding native Appalachians. The series is meant to serve as a resource, an eye-opener, a declaration of independence, a source of reference to the progress that has occurred in Appalachia, by showcasing its finest writers, poets and singer/songwriters.

Kari Gunter-Seymour
Executive Director
Women of Appalachia Project

Bianca X

What Women Do

We say, Here, take this.
Take this ___________ .
Line it with legends and long-lost treasure maps.
Whatever points to adventure and you.
We say, Here, take this, too.
Take my ___________ .
Fill it up with sparrow bones and screws,
leaves of aloe, antler tips, horseshoes, and cabochons.
Anything about you that's been unmade,
in this ___________ right here, will be made new.
We say, Here, I haven't used this ___________
in a very long time—I don't even know
how it works anymore.
Go ahead, rip open the seams.
Let's see what it looks like inside out.
We say, Stretch this. We say, Tighten that.
We say, You're squeezing too hard.
We say, Don't ever let go.
We say, I don't need much. Take this ___________.
And this ___________.
And this ___________.
But you don't want any of those things.
What you want more than the geode of us,
more than the starlit gospel of us,
more than the low-hanging plum of us,
more than anything we might give away for free,
is whatever we mean when we say,
But not this ___________.
You can't ever, ever, take this from me.

Please.

Don't take this ___________ away.

The Woman is Round

The woman
is round the way he likes,
and her hair is the aurora borealis
and her teeth are phantoms
in selenite and her clavicle
is a tomb in which he thinks
he would like to
enshroud his lips,
and her garment is a forsythia bush
slipping from her right shoulder,
so when she turns to look back at him,
he can make out the birthmark on her
back which is a mammatocumulus
cloud, adrift,
and her spine is a haint-blue bottle
dangling from a limb, and her gaze
is the New Testament, and her left temple
is a grove of pear trees, and the scar above her
upper lip is a pier where she docks
11:11 wishes, and her beauty mark is a mantis
trapped in amber, and her ears
are hyacinth blooms,
and the tops of her breasts
are waves cresting at dusk,
and her knuckles are hard candy,
and her scent is that of a newborn fawn
or the underside of a pawpaw tree leaf,
and her dreams are jelly jars crammed
with stag beetles and butterfly wings
and opossum bones and upper rooms,
but he finds he can't ever touch her—
his fingers slide off her skin which is a
crazy quilt of rainbow light spun
from prisms—no matter how
tightly he closes
his fist.

Bianca X

To the Woman I Saw Today Who Wept in Her Car

Woman,
I get it.
We are strangers,
but I know the heart is a hive,
and someone has knocked yours
from its high branch in your chest
and it lays cracked and splayed,
spilling honey all over
the ground floor of your gut,
and the bees inside
that you've trained
over the days and years
to stay put, swarm
the terrain of your organs,
yes,
right here in traffic,
while we wait for the light to change.

I get it.
How this array of metal and plastic
tends to go womb room
once the door shuts,
and maybe you were singing
only moments before
you got the call,
or remembered that thing
you had tucked back and built
such sturdy scaffolding all around,
and now here it comes to knock
you adrift with only your steering
wheel to hold you up.

Or, maybe today
was just a tough day,
and the sunlight,
and warm weather,
and blossoming limbs,
and smiling pedestrians

waiting for their turn to cross
are much too much to take
when you think of all that's left
in this day, and here you are,
a reed stuck in the mud
of a rush hour intersection,
with so very many hours left to go.

Woman,
I know you.
I know how that thing
when left unattended
will show up as a typhoon
on your front door
demanding to be let in,
or it will take
the whole damn house with it.

I know this place, too.
I get it.

And because we are strangers,
because you did not see me see you,
my gaze has no more effect
than a specter who stares at the living.
And yet, I want you to know that
today, in the hive of my heart,
there is room enough
for you.

ODANA CHANEY

Babylon Was Built on a Riverbank

Ezekiel 36:25 Then will I sprinkle clean water upon you, and ye shall be clean: from all your filthiness, and from all your idols, will I cleanse you.

In the Lord's Year 2016, we forgot that God hasn't been to these mountains since he made them.

We prayed and prayed to find that baby boy swept away by muddy waters, to find the man who was washed asunder when he went lookin'. That's the year we prayed our loved ones were safe, the year we watched the water spill over dams as if they were doorsteps. In the Lord's Year 2016, we had no spirit inside us left to be surprised or angry or anything but tired when the bridges were carried away, the year when 44 of 55 counties declared emergency for the rain that rolled off the backs of mountains and filled in every valley we had the audacity to call civilized. There was a woman taken by the creek when she climbed and clawed her way from dog pen to dog pen in her holler, unchaining abandoned hounds too scared to even bay. My Papaw always said you can learn everything you need to know about a person by how they treat their dogs.

No cries of grief echo off these hills, the mist sits as still as your Ma in her living room watching the pretty faces on the news talk about the third hundred-year flood we've had this decade. In the Lord's Year 2016, we did what we always do and stood like stone-coal as a woman watched her house float down a rushing pop-up river, broken, in a thousand pieces, and on fire. That river, like the mud caked to our hearts, was not there yesterday. In that year we didn't even cry or howl: we buried our dead in silence, knowing that we were lucky to even have bodies to put in the soggy ground. We remembered those abandoned hounds in that forsaken holler, wondering…if we are the ones who are left, who was the hunter who left us?

Joy Duffy

Ellie Mayday

Tina Parker

Exodus

I

I pull the first one from my mouth
My body blooms holes
Open wounds
Snakes come out in droves

II

A school bus takes
The children
We climb Stop signs
But cannot find them

III

A crack in the wall down
Down the fissure grows
The gaping hole cannot hold
No one is safe at home

IV

Police line up
Row after row
Say each name
So many kinds
Of cancer

TINA PARKER

Radiation Therapy: A Baptism

I wear a white robe
It billows on the water
The pastor pinches my nostrils
His palm covers my mouth
The water holds me
The ones I love are with me
I take Jesus into my heart

The tumor is over my heart
Plastic plugs my nostrils
A plastic tube in my mouth
I listen for the voice
On the intercom

*Take a deep breath
and hold it*

I inhale and lift my ribcage
Light soaks my chest
The great machine takes me
Deep into the wilderness
No one can come with me

You can breathe

****

*Take a deep breath
and hold it*

I summon a river
A rippling current
And halos of light
The Holy Spirit descends
As a heron
O Spirit stay with me I plead
The voice calls me back

You can breathe

And I breathe.

TINA PARKER

Reading the Obits

I keep a tally
Mostly they live
A long time

One woman my age
Died at the hospice care center
A childhood friend died
Peacefully at home

I look for ratios
For patterns
A way to measure
Or predict

The woman's voice is kind
But firm
On the cancer care app
She says I will get well
For the joy of living
But I thrive on the fear
Of dying.

VICKI PRITCHARD

Upon my Back: Black in Appalachia

I'm thankful. I got a job, and it's a real callin'. I graduated top of the nurse aid class; yep, I did. Old folks, they need care, and I can give it. Sometimes they sweet, sometimes they cuss me. Humpf, an' when they do, they remember that "N" word.

Hey, 'scuse me while I straighten up. My old back is groanin'. Can you really see me? Well, I'm part of this place too. But man oh man, is it ever a struggle.

The old black men and the old white ones too, they don't care 'bout my skin, long as I come when called and can sing a George Jones song. Ya know, me and my ol' man, we went all the way to the Grand Ole Opry to see Lonesome George. Now, ain't that a Appalachian hoot?

That lead aide, ol' Rosie, she says the fact so many of us girls is black, gives the owner the right to keep us all in low wages. She says Appalachian women got it rough anyway and them rich owners just wear one out and run another'n in. Well, boohoo. Poor her.

You ask me, whatever them as in power wants to be Appalachian, well, that's what it is. It ain't me, I guess. Oh, I got the back for it, and I got the almighty national origin. What I ain't got is the consent. Still, it's in my veins, I reckon.

My favorite patient, Miz Jenkins…she a hundred and one. She be like a queen to me. No recollection in her ol' days of drugs and guns. She safe in church, the black church, a-course. I never miss neither, 'cause with all my own there, I can be me. Ain't no need to cross over that bridge with them blue eyes. Can't pay the toll no-ways.

At church, for a little while, I forget about the politics. I think my kids'll be strong and happy; not full of drugs and maybe gettin' killed. For a little while, I feel like we all goin' to be ok in the end. I feel like I really can earn enough money, someday.

Yeah, yeah, I can get lots of overtime work, but I got to add it up right. I got a lot of kin to feed. The money just ain't enough to risk my supplement.

Oh, let me rub my old back some more. They's no end to the lifts, the twists. We got mechanical machines, but they scare the ol' folks. Lots of 'em, they like to hold to a real person. Sometimes, my old back… I lift, we lift, my team of mates, my girls. That's what they call us, "girls."

Ol' blond-headed Rosie, she say we all in the same boat…with no oars, and it ain't even our boat. My mates, we kiss and hug and love on all the poor old folks. We keep 'em in the boat. That boat be our life-boat too.

Rosie, her mouth gonna get her in trouble. Plus, she plain lazy…hold'n back 'til I get there. That mouthy Rosie says, "hey girl, we're all n------ here." Humpf. Not true, she Appalachian.

EMALEA NEAL RUPE

Evening Blue

Hope Against Hope

1

My mother came to her marriage with a wooden trunk she called a hope chest, a gift when she graduated from Prestonsburg High School, in Eastern Kentucky. The chest was a classic in its day. Made by the Lane Company of Altavista, Virginia, it was a serviceable five by two-foot rectangular, lidded box made of light and dark red cedar. The hope chest eventually came to our house in the state capitol, Frankfort, where I lived as a child.

When I looked at the chest, I turned that word, *hope,* over and oer inside my mouth, and it was bittersweet. Still, my father, who loved reading history, lent the hope chest a kind of glamor. Our family came from Germany, from Ireland, some from the mountains of Spain, he said, and in those places, they called hope chests dowries. Trousseaus. Glory boxes. Some of those chests, he said, were fancy. Painted with gold leaf or hand carved to relay stories from the girl's family. The chests could be tall, double-doored, or smaller boxes with intricate enamels, all made to hold the prized possessions and household goods a woman saved for her marriage. My father loved summoning stories, and he filled the hope chests he told me about with silks and embroidered slippers, gloves made from rabbit fur, velvet slippers. And didn't I know, he exclaimed, there was a hope chest found inside the walls at my granny's house when that new room was added. That hope chest mostly held letters and deeds, but also a china-faced doll with wooden teeth, and, he claimed, a petticoat stained with the blood of an unfaithful woman who had been shot by her lover.

Years later, I wrote about that hope chest, filled it with my imaginings of the ghosts of the women who were my ancestors. *Nethaladia. Exer. Armentia George.* For my mother, the hope chest was just plain furniture, polished just as much as everything else in our spotless house. She laid a starched doily across its top, and on that kept a black plastic bowl painted with bamboo, something my father had brought back from Korea. I imagined that the chest was a little like Pandora's box, except that it sat in a corner of my parent's bedroom, where I never saw it opened.

2

The first lines of one of Emily Dickinson's most well-known poems, written in 1861, is about hope. *That thing with feathers*, she writes, *that perches in the soul…sings the tune without the words.* The poem is an extended metaphor, likening hope to a feathered bird permanently perched in the soul of every human. There it sings, never stopping in its quest to inspire. Emily Dickinson wrote the poem in 1862, one of nearly 1800 poems she penned during her lifetime, only seven of which were published. Her poems, together with those of Walt Whitman, are called pioneering works that point the way to a new era of poetry in the English-speaking world.

And yet, after a lifetime of reading the poem again and again, of taping copies of it above years of writing desks, of reclaiming it again and again in my memory, I continue not to find the poem particularly hopeful. Hope, that stalwart bird, that ceaseless singer, perches, sings without words, keeps so many warm, but is an inhabitant of chilly lands. My mind's eye sees bedraggled feathers, sees a beak beneath a wing, sees the frailty of bird bones beneath, shivering wet plumes. And what kind of bird? Gull, starling, grackle, dove? I want to take the little bird in, name it. Hold it next to my chest until it is again dry fluff, but that contradicts my essential discomfort with the poem in the first place. The bird sings sweetly for others, keeps others warm, never stops, never stops. I am such a woman. She who sings others safe. She who survives storm, storm, storm, but remains stalwart. She who takes in, asks nothing, surrenders her own hope in deference to this one, that one, the other. Even as I recite the poem today, I feel a trace of down sticking in my throat.

3

My mother's hope chest was a mystery, as were other things in our house. My mother's wedding rings had been bought in Morocco, when my father was in the Air Force. I had only seen the wedding rings a few times, as these were kept in a drawer somewhere in my parent's bedroom, since my mother said her hands, rough and red with cleaning up after us, were not meant for diamonds. My father had also brought home an elaborate set of china—all the fixings, from cups and saucers, to plates small and large—said to be "stored" in a box in our crawl-space, but I had never seen it. And in the garage, where I had to stay each afternoon after school until my mother let me come inside, was the greatest mystery. On top of a tall metal cabinet, a large box, said to hold photographs from my father's years in the Korean War.

My mother, when asked about the box, said she'd never allow such things to come inside any house of hers. One afternoon, I tried to reach the box. An aluminum, fold-out ladder took me to the top of the work bench next to the cabinet, and I juggled the box down. I knelt on the work bench as I pried the snug cardboard top open with a screwdriver. Slides. There were boxes and boxes of them, each labeled in my father's neat handwriting. *Seoul. Air Base. Daegu.* At random, I opened the box labeled Seoul, and held a slide to the light. A woman, the nipples of her bare breasts covered with sequins, danced on a narrow stage, her arms stretched above her head, her lips parted in a way that made me shiver. A room below her was crowded with uniformed men, their expressions a mixture of laughter and surprising rage. I thought I saw my father in the room, a boy-version of him, but as hard as I tried, I couldn't recognize his face.

4

Hope, according to the OED, has its origins with the late Old English *hopa,* a noun, and the Germanic *hopian,* a verb. Popular phrases including the word hope: hope against hope; hope springs eternal; not a hope. Among the colloquialisms I grew up with: *About as much hope as an ice cube in hell. You just go right ahead and hope.* And lastly, according to Urban Thesaurus, the top five slang words for hope: von; gmh (gives me hope); invader zim (one's last hope); hiv (hope is vital); and juggalo holocaust (the hope for our future). There are one thousand four hundred and three other words related to the concept of hope.

5

I tried more than once to slip into their bedroom to open the chest, but the Lane hope chest was built with a traditional design: a self-locking lid, and it held tight. I imagined what might be inside. When I was very small, my mother had Melmac dinnerware—a mixture of pink plates and black cups, the colors Elvis favored. I imagined delicate pink glasses inside the chest, ones with stems I could twirl between my fingers, unlike all the glasses I was never allowed to touch in the kitchen. I imagined luminous shakers, pink glass, the salt inside tinged rose. Oh! And the things that could be black! Shining paperweights. Miniature black dogs, glass dogs like the real ones I wanted but wasn't allowed. What else might the hope chest hold? Stacks of records, maybe, all of them Frank Sinatra, my mother's favorite. Had she had enchanted evenings? Silk blouses. Slinky lace slips. Dresses as green as my mother's eyes. Dresses she might have worn when she was young.

Had she ever been a girl, part of the world of girls, wished-for boys, laughter? Had my mother been young, once upon a time? Had she been young in my father's arms? Young enough to wish on stars in a cold winter sky. Young enough to hope against hope that the world might turn out okay. Young enough to fill a hope chest with all the things that might be and not the way they could have been. Her eyes now were narrowed, her face shadowed with a thing I didn't know how to name.

6

A passed down story in my childhood concerned a fireplace. The fireplace had long since been boarded up, a gas heater installed in its stead, but the story brought it back to life. My Granny Baisden, my mother's mother, loved cautionary tales, ones short and long. Don't wash your hair during your period, she'd say. Don't look twice at a black cat. Don't think about going with him, she'd say to my Aunt Ruby, who was courting a wild man who drank and was said to drive a racy car, feet on the steering wheel. My mother was a good girl, she said, but she still married that service man who'd been to all those foreign countries, then took her as far away as Topeka, Kansas, her pregnant while they drove all those miles. Who knew what living in a place no one ever heard of did to a body, and then he got out of the Air Force and up and moved her where no one could reach her, and what about that?

The story about the fireplace was no less forbidding.

A long time ago, another girl used to live in the house my mother was raised in. *A girl a little older than you, missy,* my grandmother said.

I was sitting on the green, horsehair sofa, holding her hairpins while she combed and braided her waist-length hair.

That girl dreamed big. Dreamed about foreign places. Cities up north. Dreamed about big, fine cars, and sweet water running in the kitchen, and roads and roads she had no business taking. *Her dreams were too big for her britches,* she said as I snuggled next to her, put my head on her knee.

The girl did her dreaming in front of the fireplace, chock full of coal and kindling, burning and hot. She was sitting and rocking in a chair with her eyes closed and paying no mind at all. It was cold of a winter, too, the winds whistling up the hollow, winds that softened and bent as they wrapped their selves around the house. A winter song that nigh about sung her to sleep. Who knew what the wind-sound really was—the voice of God humming down from the sky, maybe, warning her about what was what? *And before she knew it, she'd fell forward right into the fire. Face first, her hands out trying to stop her, but it was nary a bit of use.*

The rest of the story was a warning like all the smaller ones about hair washing or mirrors or birds flying into the house. The girl's face was badly scarred. Some even said the scar —one purplish-red and covering the right side of her face—was in the shape of a large hand. That could have meant about anything. *Warning, warning. Stop.* Here the story branched off into possibilities. (a) She never married, had to go on living at home on and on. (b) She ran around with who knows who and took up drinking and what not and you know what that means (c) She caught herself just before she fell, and things went forward much as expected.

The Girl Who Fell into the Fire became a kind of moral and empirical code that my mother and her sisters and I were to live by. Don't dream too big, now. Watch yourselves. Don't hope for too much.

7

Some of the first books I remember were the ones my mother told me she'd read in high school—the Sue Barton series. *Sue Barton: Student Nurse. Senior Nurse. Staff Nurse.* The books show our heroine, Sue, as she undertakes medical training, then enters her career—all the while meeting, then marrying, her husband-to-be, Dr. Bill Barry. Along the way, of course, Sue manages to have adventures. She falls down a laundry chute. Saves a feverish patient from jumping out of a window while recovering from appendix surgery. Sue is loyal and unrelentingly kind. At one point she sells her wedding clothes so that an elderly patient who wants to travel can fulfill her dreams. After marriage, she works in a New York City settlement house, then as a visiting rural nurse in the midst of a typhoid epidemic. When we last see Sue, she has returned to work to support her four children while her husband Bill is in a sanatorium, suffering from tuberculosis. I read each of these books cover to cover less in search of who I might someday become, and more in search of who my mother was and why.

Pearlie Lee Baisden was known as Perky Pearlie in high school, the girl with rolled down bobby sox and a tendency, even then, toward perfection. She pin-curled her hair with precision, ironed her blouses and pleated her pedal pushers. Her father wouldn't let her date, met her and whoever at the bottom of the hill with a shotgun, but still there was this one boy who gave her his class ring to wrap yarn around so it fit for a while. At eighteen she graduated, worked as a waitress at a drive-in in Allen, Kentucky, where she met my father, just before he joined the Air Force, and went overseas. From there he wrote her letters. *Every time I see another girl, the first thing I do is compare them to you, you are so far ahead of them I'd darn near be ashamed to go out with them.* Marriage at twenty. A child at twenty-two. A trailer in Harlan County, where she lived while my father taught high school algebra. Another trailer back in Allen. Then a house in Frankfort, Kentucky. How her floors gleamed, all the while photographs show her deterioration.

The narrowed eyes. The stunned look as she holds the crying baby. The fear in her eyes as they moved to one place, then another, when she'd never much been beyond the world of her parents in Dwale, Kentucky. Tight lips as she stood beside me on the driveway of the house, while my father took our picture. Clean rooms. Clean floors. Chairs to look at, never sit in. Tables with food we ate carefully, never touching it with our hands. My father, working late at the office, and those calls from some woman. *I sleep with your husband two or three times a week.* Her hope chest had opened like Pandora's box and all the wishes flew out, their dark wings folding her in until she grew smaller and smaller and smaller.

8

The summer I was ten or eleven, I grew fascinated with the hope chest's lock. My mother spent hours in the bathroom by then, making up her face, washing her hair, and that gave me time for covert missions. I was a spy. An adventurer. I Silently opened the refrigerator, slipped out one slice of the full pack of cheese. Stole cereal from the box, all the while making sure nothing rustled. Grew bold enough to slide drawers open without a sound, where I took out and refolded underwear and shirts over which I had no province. I broke every rule of my mother's orderly dominion.

Like that, I revisited the hope chest. Pressed the lock's button in, held it there, pushed up on the chest's lid. Nothing. Pressed again. Click, loud enough to make my heart race. Again. Press, hold, lift. Still nothing. From outside the bedroom door and down the hall, sounds from the bathroom. The AM radio playing. *Do you know the way to San Jose? I've been away so long. I may go wrong and lose my way.* I heard my mother coughing, then water running in the sink. Safe. I pressed again. Hold, lift. This time, the top of the chest opened, and I gasped, holding my breath against the creak, creak as I raised the lid inch by inch.

I remembered all the historic possibilities my father had described for hope chests. Silks and embroidered pillow cases. What were the equivalent possibilities? Blankets and quilts too good for our beds. Glass boxes of bath powders and tiny pots of eye shadow in amber and brilliant green. Clothes my mother wore when she was in high school—the plaid skirts and elbow-length sweaters she had me wear to school now. Or the chest held more of what I'd seen as I snuck into the drawer of their bedside table. Square foil pouches marked Trojan or the book with a cheerleader in a garter belt on the cover that my mother had found underneath the sink in my father's bathroom. I hoped briefly it was none of these things, but something soft, beautiful. Something rose-colored, pink, pale blue. I closed my eyes a minute and made a wish for this thing, though I could not begin to imagine what it might be.

As the years passed, I would be able to conjure it very exactly, that scent of cedar and must. I'd be able to see the red striations of the wood, the four corners. Clean and plain. Polished. No dusty surface to leave my marks, and other than that, nothing at all. The hope chest was empty.

9

Once I was out on my own, I went years without calling her or visiting her or acknowledging her in any way. I wanted to exorcise her. Expunge the memory of her hands cleaning sinks, floors, walls, me. Forgetting. I wanted to forget my mother's sad eyes, her relentless anger over why my father, at last, had divorced her. I wanted most of all to forget that I'd had a mother who hugged me by keeping her body rigid, away from all contact, the embrace translated to a brief pat and release. Did she love me? I had cards and letters that said so. *Merry Christmas. Love, Mother.* Cards piled up in a box, and the rooms of all the houses I lived in were cluttered with these snippets of affection. When I finally resumed visiting her, I often sat at her kitchen table and licked Top Value Stamps into a book while she rehearsed the past. Had he loved her? Did I really believe there was such a thing as love? Were there enough stamps yet to get her a new vacuum cleaner? Eventually, she fell ill with Alzheimer's. Before she died, she forgot everything, even how to breathe.

When my mother asked again and again about love in those last years, I want to think this was a translation of what she had always wanted so badly. She'd had a blank space inside her chest, and she'd believed with all her heart that some boy, a boy, then the boy who was my father would know just how to fill up her life. With boys came houses, and with houses came dishware and soap operas on weekday afternoons. With houses came windows lit up at night with a family watching television shows about happy families, and then and then. Then came the pause. The shoe that fell with no other shoe afterwards, and what to do then? Had she not tried hope? Why, look at it. That chest in the corner of their room, and she'd wanted to fill it up, hadn't she? She'd meant to fold all the little towels, the sheets and the monogramed pillow cases and the quilts, but time had passed and she hadn't quite done what she'd planned and so she brought to their marriage like it was. And thus time passed. Who was I to say that look in her eyes at the end of her life was empty? Who was I to say there wasn't such a thing as hope against hope.

10

These days my mother's hope chest sits at the foot of my own bed. I have filled it with one of the things I love most. Quilts. The quilts were made years ago by my father's mother, and they are the patterns I love most. Trip Around the World. Log Cabin. Cathedral Window. More than the patterns, I love knowing where the cloth came from. Some of it repurposed from the Mountain Mission Store or from her love of yard sales. Much of the cloth, though, is a repository of history. The square of blue cloth from an apron. A brown square from a dress I remembered wearing in third grade. A sky-blue square from a blouse, a favorite of my mother's once upon a time. The quilts are a gathering—my girlhood; moments from my mother's married life; snippets from my grandmother's life; pieces after piece from the lives of women whose names I will never know. The quilts are an accumulation of stories, much like essays that operate nonlinearly. As Sarah Minor says in "What Quilting and Embroidery Can Teach Us About Narrative Time," some essays (like the braid or the collage) are made of "threads" that combine to form a complete and pliable piece of nonfiction, gathered pieces that don't abide by chronological time. I choose to see those quilts as a kind of living hope.

I, myself, have often not been a beacon of hopefulness, or even of much faith at all. I've lived sometimes what seems a hundred lives. Jobs. States. Lovers. Nothing has been a standing ground, nothing lasting too long. I've moved east to west to avoid heartache. Changed license plates rather than making a decision about love. Tossed a way of life out the window like a cigarette butt on the highway, liking the way the sparks shattered, a pretty breaking as I kept on driving past. And don't get me started on God. Her. Him. Buddhist. Episcopalian. Quaker. God's face in my mind is so multifaceted, I haven't been able to make a clear choice, except for the images of the Holy Mother that appear as candles and icons in most of the rooms I call my own.

As clearly as I have liked transiency, be it of the heart or the spirit, a thread has followed me, stitching together this year with that one, this life with one I've left behind. On road trips sometimes, I'll look at my face in the sideview mirror, and see her face, my mother's, instead of my own. The same sad eyes, the same half smile. My choices are so dissimilar from hers, and yet there she is, looking back at me from out of my very own face. Do I harbor a secret wish for the good Doctor Bob from the Sue Barton books to sweep down out of the sky and set my car on the right road toward marriage and family? Not that, exactly, but surely, I have longed for a center. A light in the middle of the dark forests in which I have placed myself, liking the restlessness, the home always outside my reach.

Like the center of each block in the Log Cabin quilt. The red or yellow square that makes the brightest place amid the all the other lines that make the cabins. That's the quilt on top when I open the hope chest these days. I'm not saying I hear voices exactly when I open that chest, but maybe. The quilts are made of voices and times and places. They are bits and pieces of other lives handed down to me, some of them women's lives. My mother's story is there, as is mine, and when I open the chest the scent of cedar rises to me, warm and alive. The stories are there as I open this quilt or that one, wrap it around me, hold on.

Connaught Cullen

Tricolor Wood

Linda Parsons

Contrary

Blessed are the contrary, accent on the second syllable in mid-
South talk—as my sainted grandmother let fly when I ragged on
about Polly's market, bartered dime to quarter for candy cigarettes.
Contrary at the edge of my mother's serration, my sass not to dispute
her word. Contrary like a pressure cooker's spew of soupbeans
on the wallpaper after years of lightly, lightly on eggshells.
Not *have a blessed day*, but blessed be contrariness for the sake
of my brain and mouth and voice that won't be shushed, even
by my ownself. My ownself that rents sackcloth at the mirror
of *mea culpas* for things this mouth upended. Contrary, not
meaning meanness or gossip or mock, but a by God honest tongue.
Woe to them that can't meet on the dotted line, toe to toe, can't
pick that bone to the blood heart, where the rubber meets the real.
Call it age or a confluence of contrariness, rivered down
the ancestral stream. Above all, let me be kind, let me deliver
the biscuits and butter of kindness in a wicker basket clothed
in linen to the least of us, love as its double cousin—no cheek
to turn, stone to unturn, no backtalk to walk back—just a table
polished with Pledge, just as I am with only one plea: to be
and be heard, all of me neither sour nor sweet, then to lean in
close, and lean closer, to listen.

Valerie Nieman

Black Pudding

Catch every drop of blood
when you slice the squeal.

Gather it up with oats
pilfered from the miller's share;
eke it out with suet
cut from around the heart.

Employ every bit of the beast,
the gullet, the ribbons of gut,
siphon the air from its lungs,
the last belch from its belly.

Hang your black sausages
in the attic, pickle the trotters
and smoke the hams. Hope there's
enough for the long nights,

pray that the gods won't
return for their due.

Rose M. Smith

The Harbinger

Corduroy overalls, black ones, faded dusky brown,
back pockets worn wale-free, threadbare
by your wallet on one side, tobacco tin on the other.
A blue plaid flannel shirt worn limp by years.
A carved brown pipe pocked on its rump.
Tooth marks along the mouthpiece.
These things are well remembered. How
you cradled that pipe—left hand, gently as if the back
of a baby's neck. How it dangled from your mouth
as your hoed a row in Ohio back-yard dirt.

You taught me young just where work lives.
Girl, you sho'nuff ironing, as I readied your shirts
on Saturday nights for your day on the deacons' bench.
Can't iron worth lick ain't got your shoulder hunched up.
Hardly an ounce of fat on your mahogany arms,
snake of vein lacing muscle rendered hard by labor,
you and your Bible such familiar sight. There—
on the back steps, there—on the patio's rusty swing.
You'd read that massive yellowed book
til 10 dressed the clock and we all hunkered, quiet
so you could fall asleep.

Now here you are in the chair no one uses anymore,
a specter back to show what hard work is, warning
to lay off the cigarettes or end up in St. Somebody's
semi-private room, lungs too black and phlegm-filled
for anyone to save, coal-miner lungs bought
one package at a time. Don't know why
God would lend you back to me. Would not have
Believed 'til I woke to the smell of that tobacco
you tamped down for years,
saw something, there in the semi dark,
in soft-wale, one hand on that antique Bible,
unmistakable voice commanding me, *Hunch up.*

Rose M. Smith

Night Clothes

Grandmother's nightgown came to me at twenty-four
with heirlooms wrapped in plastic.
Translucent white on my brown skin,
I loved the way it whispered secrets to my years
and flowed around my bare feet, begged to be filled.

I let its soft lace lie against the lactate wish
of rivers not yet flowing and whispered cleavage
where only a wish had been once hidden.
I doubled it around me, crushed its folds
in trembling, sweaty palms.

Alone in the stucco at fourteen, I opened the drawer
in her room to finger the crinkle woven in
by souls who heard the song of these synthetic fibers' wales,
imagined fineries of my own but none so grand
and wondered often why she failed to wear them.

Grandmother's nightgown came in search of my small frame
just days after the limousines pulled away.
I was elected, chosen, worried then
what spirits would come softly in the drape
to change my youth forever.

Not so early it might fall to the suckle,
be stained by letdown or by babes.
Not so late the queenly flow of manmade blends
might go unnoticed in the dim of many days.
Grandmother's nightgown came to me

Before her waist became my waist,
before the droop, before the spread,
before her pout had settled deeply into my own chin.
Before my face became her face without the Alabama burn.
Before the lace began to show its age.

If I had seen what promise lay within its seams
would I have found it still so great a treasure?

Handed both my future and my past
would I still so quickly answer *yes* and take it
when they ask?

How To Make An Appalachian Woman

Mix the disappointment with the meal,
fry it up good,
darken the edges,
add a bad joke to cope, call it cornbread.

Soften macaroni in tomatoes,
make sure to leave the skin,
call it resilience.

Pinto beans. From a can.
No, really, just pinto beans.
And humility.

Green beans, and some dead
pig pieces
because the men of the family
insist on a hint of grief.

Mash the potatoes down deep in the pot
because you know what's best for them;
because your grandmother showed you how
and that's what love is -
suffocating, rich, with pepper
every now and then,
when you've got the energy to spare
on suffering the burn.

KELSIE TYSON

Pantyhose

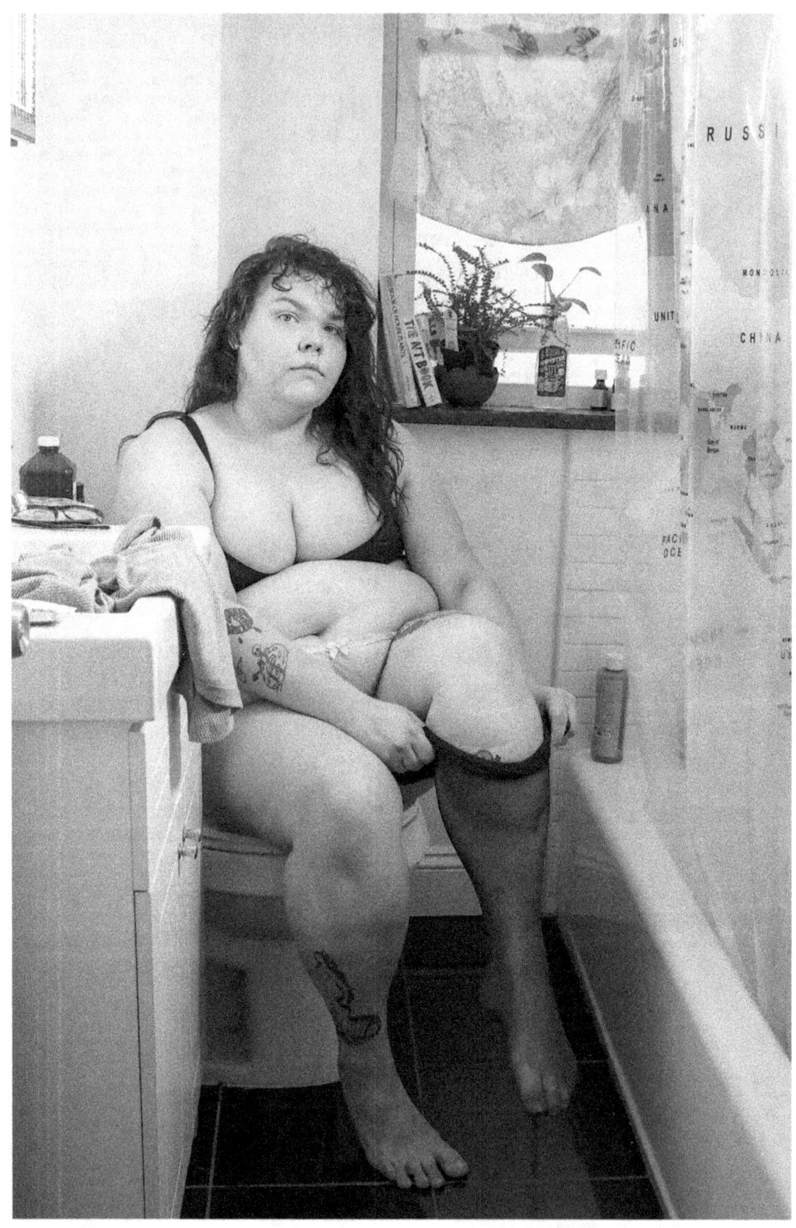

Kristine Williams

Frisson

you explain,
six feet of lanky, loose-jointed boy
slouched in the passenger seat,
finger stabbing at the console,
that feeling at the end of *this* song
shatters my spine.
Do you ever feel like that, Mom?

And I bite my tongue
but in my head I make a list:
the first time I saw your long fingers,
the way your hair curls over your collar
no matter how many times
you wet and comb it,
the time I saw you hold that girl's face
framing it with your hands
before you leaned in
and I turned away.
Every day I know you.

I don't say it,
but I wish I had.

KRISTINE WILLIAMS

Hunting Abalone

You tell a story that starts
just before dawn, and I see
stars bright still, horizon indigo,
remember a dress that color,
dancing with the boy who asked me
at the last minute,
saved me,
held me against his body,
tender new breasts in my first strapless bra.

Thirty years later, your voice
takes me to the rocks,
coast of Point Reyes,
no sunbathing here, just you,
reaching blindly under jagged rock in,
not even faith, just wanting,
searching lightly,
questing fingers gentle and quick,
brushing along to feel for the
foot of abalone there.
Reach wrong or roughly
and the muscle will clench around your hand,
trapping you, tide rising.
Divers have drowned that way.
The water is cold, you say,
so you drink brandy,
and I feel the fiery track it makes
from the back of your throat
to your stomach, warmth spreading.
Later, on the beach, there is a fire,
your friend pounding the abalone,
cooking it so tender you could scoop it
with the edge of your spoon.

I think of the boy who promised in the dark,
left me after graduation,
disappeared to Alaska,
left me scooped out, tender.

That blue dress hung on the back of the closet door
for two years, until I left for college,
wondering about the boy who made my heart clench.
I would have drowned that way.

Mimi Railey Merritt

Unveiling

In the West Virginia mountains, we sleep in July with windows open to mate-calling tree frogs at night and birdsong at dawn. Roses, hydrangeas and purple-blossomed hostas do not fear a pandemic, much less the bees that suck their sugar. Nature is healthy, we are advised. Take walks, dine outside, garden. No mask needed in my own backyard.

But I venture out weekly for groceries, my face masked and my car stocked with Clorox wipes and hand sanitizer. I see others as I shop, mostly unmasked, and I worry they are judging me: they think I'm afraid, weak, politically unattractive.

I used to smile at people I passed in the aisles. Before the pandemic, strangers would approach me in the wine aisle. "My doctor said I should drink wine for my heart," the conversation might begin. "Which wine is good?" I was flattered; I must be approachable. Now, I'm the stranger, hiding behind my mask, attempting warmth without a grin. It's a new term, I've read: smeyesing, smiling with eyes only.

It's not enough.

A friend from church called. Our church stopped in-person services for three months but recently resumed. I haven't been attending, too scared still of group gatherings, even though masks are required and physical distancing is enforced in an every-other-pew strategy.

"Didn't I see you, last Sunday?" he asked. "Oh," he replied when I answered no. "I thought it was you. You just can't tell who anyone *is* anymore, behind these masks. I met a visitor two Sundays ago and asked if she had a photograph of herself. She looked confused – that is, her *eyes* looked confused – and I explained I wanted to see her face so I could remember her."

And I thought about the person he had thought was me: who is my masked twin? Who has my hair and my eyes, or smeyes, but not necessarily my nose, lips or chin.

I'm growing too accustomed to my mask. I wonder if I will I ever unmask. Last fall I was in a different quarantine, sequestered at my 95-year-old mother's sick bed, which devolved into her deathbed, afraid of missing the last breath.

She had delivered me into my first breath, drawing back a veil for me to enter this life, and now here was I, pushing spoonfuls of applesauce and sips of water as she readied herself to leave this life for the next. Even as she talked increasingly to someone in the shadows beyond me and above me, her words in those moments unintelligible, I couldn't leave her alone.

The hospice nurse authorized a dose of morphine if necessary; methadone might become insufficient as the pancreatic cancer violated the peaceful calm that was her strength. Already the disease had invaded her body, spreading to stomach and spine and descending through hip bones.

She was dying, but she was not losing her mind. One day she asked for her notebook, the one in which she had itemized her possessions: furniture, rugs, paintings, wedding china and crystal, the sterling silver flatware passed down to her from her grandmother. She had signed a will years ago, but it was simple, dividing everything equally among my two brothers, my sister and me. The notebook was the real document. She had opened it countless times in recent years to make notes as we sipped wine together while watching sunsets.

On this day, she wanted to ensure I knew her instructions, and we went through every item, checking that all the histories were recorded: the corner cupboard was made on her grandfather's farm in the 1800s ("My people were gifted woodworkers," she reminded me); "The Red Poppies" she had painted herself, winning a third place ribbon at a regional art show; the Wedgewood china with the vivid rose and blue flowers she had selected as a bride.

On another day, she asked for her jewelry box.

I shuddered. "Not now," I said. "Later. Let's do it this weekend, when family comes in." The diagnosis had meant a steady streaming in and out of loved ones, eager to share stories, thinking goodbyes if not voicing them. Fresh cut flowers, homemade custards, and hands holding hers were a luxury of dying before the pandemic.

"I need to get this straight," she insisted.

I brought her the box, and she, too weak to rummage through bracelets and rings, watched me pull out the strand of pearls she'd worn on her wedding day and the gold charm bracelet that had distracted fussy grandchildren.

"No," she said. "Not those. Keep looking…for the small diamond."

I put back into the box the pearls, the charm bracelet, and the big diamond ring Daddy bought her for their 50th anniversary.

I checked the top drawer of her dresser. There, in a tiny velvet pouch, was a diamond ring so small I could not imagine it ever slipping over the arthritis-swollen joint of my mother's ring finger.

"That's the one," she said.

I handed it to her, and she held it up to the light. Though her hearing was diminished, even with powerful aids, her eyesight had never failed her, a blessing for one who loved to read, to sketch faces and to catch sunlight filtering through pine trees.

"This was the first ring your father gave me," she said. "It's not worth much. His mother spent the paychecks he sent home from the war."

I remembered the family history: my grandmother, Nana, wringing her hands, a widow left to raise four children in a depression. She'd worked two jobs, but still sometimes a child would be sent to live with cousins. Daddy worked his way through college and went to law school on the GI Bill. But the money he sent home from WWII for Nana to deposit in his savings account, she'd needed. Not much was left for an engagement ring.

"I never had enough sympathy for Nana," Mama said, looking at the ring. "A single, working mother all those dark years."

This ring, she said, should go to Caroline, the youngest grandchild, my daughter, the only one yet to settle down, the one who slept beside her grandmother on holidays and summer visits.

Then came the day we transferred Mama from her antique cherry bed to a hospital bed. When a grandson dismantled the bed with the valance of gold flowers and green vines that had veiled her rest for half a century, he brought along his ten-year-old daughter to distract her.

Mama asked me for a painting she wanted to show her great-granddaughter. "The one of the photographer," she said.

It was a 19th century painting of a family dressed in their finest, a dog at their feet, every face smiling expectantly at an odd contraption and the man behind it, both concealed by a drape of brilliant vermilion.

"Do you know what I like about this?" she asked. "It fascinates me that an ancient art form captures a brand-new art form. And the veil controls the light that the camera lets in."

My niece smiled. I like to think she saw what my mother wanted her to see.

Mama didn't care for the hospital bed. The moment we settled her in, tucking pillows against aching hips and under swollen ankles, she looked at me, cornflower blue eyes staring into my green. "Where is my valance?" she asked.

"I'm having someone adjust it so it will fit over this new bed, just so," I lied.

She saw straight through me, sighed, and turned her head away.

The next morning was her last. Alone with her, holding her hand, I heard down deep inside her what the hospice nurse had warned of – the crackling sound of the death rattle. Her lips were moving with words I couldn't hear. Was she talking to me? Or to someone else, someone dancing in the ceiling's shadows. No valance, no veil, no mask for her anymore. I felt her leave.

I am an orphan now, at 62. I walk new territory. The dining room table I coveted for decades is now mine. It seats 12, but we don't have company these days, too risky with the virus. I also have her glass prisms. By a bare window with no blinds or drapery to filter sun's rays, these light catchers cast morning rainbows across my living room ceiling from beyond the veil.

Jessica Held

Wet Paint

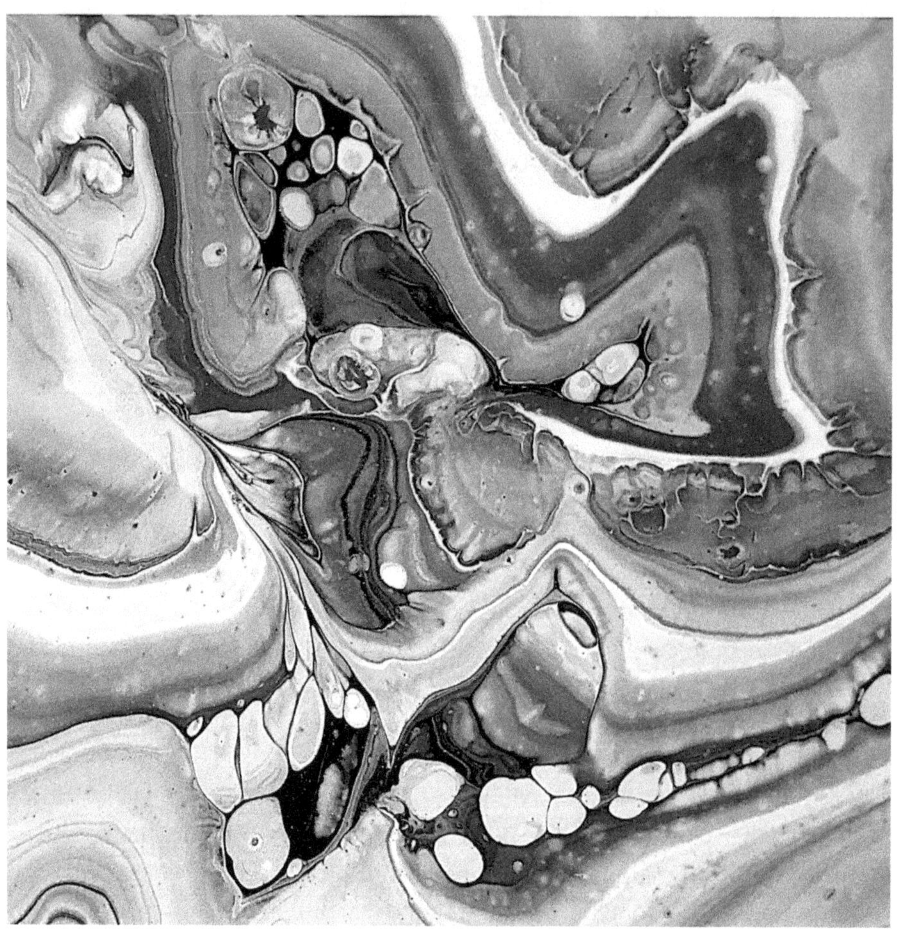

Holly Norton

Grievance

This may be morbid
But I already mourn you
Fifteen years of not speaking
Possibly forty more
People say blood is thicker than water
Our grudge is thicker than sludge in a river
We are caught on separate rocks
Holding fast to past injuries
Water rushing past like lost years.

HOLLY NORTON

Happy Ending

Those were the happy days, you said
Sock hops and bebop, Elvis the Pelvis
Saddle shoes and poodle skirts
Burgers and malts at the drive-in
Cigarettes on the sly
Cruising downtown in your dad's truck
You and your girlfriends picking up boys, taking them for rides
        til they begged you to stop.

Your yearbook said, "Good luck with Chuck," and
Right out of high school you married your sweetheart
A greaser, hair slicked back
Cigarette pack rolled up in his t-shirt
Mama's boy in motorcycle boots
Annulment after six months.

Then you took that full ride to college
Stayed for a year, got bored
Decided the big city was the place to be
You could get a job and make money
Finally be free
You saw him at the bowling alley
Company night
That swagger and sneer as he strolled down the lane
Caught your eye
You bowled a few frames
Met in the stairwell at work and necked.

Then came the 60s
California was the land of opportunity
You drove cross country
He worked at the refinery
You were at home with two babies
Made a friend who was into astrology, women's lib
Made sure he had beer in the fridge
When he came home after his shift.

He didn't like that "hippy" friend of yours
Didn't want you to go to work
Driving that bus for those disabled kids
But you did.

After that bar fight,
You wrote a letter to the judge
Told him that your husband
Was a father to small children
That you couldn't go it alone.

Then he came home after second shift
Wrapped his hands around your neck
You knew then you had to get out
Told the kids the day after Christmas
They would only be seeing him on weekends
You would be moving them back to your home.

He flew the kids first class
You drove a U-Haul from California to Iowa
Through mountains, desert, plains, to your parents
Found an apartment
Started working at the family business
Stayed up late at night
Sat in the dark, listening to The Carpenters and Dionne Warwick
Savored the quiet with the kids sleeping
Not fighting, as they did, with the neighbors complaining,
Then the eviction and the move across town.

You helped your parents build the business
Watched your brother sink it, then disappear
Leave you holding the bag
One kid in college, the other dropped out,
You moved to Florida
Cared for a father with throat cancer
Cooked and cleaned for a demanding mother
Then they were both gone and
You were alone.

The pharmacy job helped you keep the lights on
Water running and food in the fridge

The daughter visited once or twice a year
The son once, something always came up
TV, wine, and cigarettes were company
Then COPD, disability, no more being on your feet all day
You couldn't stay
Your coworkers, your only friends, threw you a party.
Then you closed the blinds, went out when you had to
People in the neighborhood wondered about you

The daughter in Ohio couldn't see you drinking or
Smoking when you took breaks from the oxygen tank
Answered your calls twice a week
Seemed too busy to listen and
You didn't want to bother her
Told her you had just a little diabetes

You fell one day, took half an hour to get up
Woke up one night not able to breathe
Called the ambulance
Congestive heart failure
You told your daughter the pillow she sent
To prop you up in bed
Was working
Even though it didn't.

A friend picked you up to give you a ride
Saw you sitting with bags on your feet
Filling up with fluid
Rushed you to the hospital
You were admitted with lymphedema.

The nurses called you the life of the party
You turned on the charm
Thanked them for all they'd done
Told your daughter you were going to get better
That you were going to live with her
She took you to rehab, and the social worker asked,
Have you had thoughts of harming yourself?
You said that you had, that you wanted to do it in the kitchen
So you wouldn't be a burden to your kids anymore.
The social workers told your daughter she better find another place for you

In case the nursing home couldn't keep you anymore.

You did the exercises they told you to
Asked your daughter to send you the Diet Coke they wouldn't take to you
She lectured you on how it wasn't good for you and that you needed to get better
So you could leave rehab and live with her.
She went back to Ohio
Called you every other night
Said you didn't sound like yourself, she couldn't understand you,
Didn't know the UTI you had did something to your mind.
But one night you said very clearly, I'm dying

They took you back to the hospital
She came back from Ohio
Took care of your bills, stayed at the house,

Sat in your hospital room as long as she could,
Listened to you moan from your hospital bed,
Watched blood from your kidneys drain into a pan
Held your hand and one day said,
I'm taking you to a place where you can let go,
Felt you squeeze her hand harder than you ever had,
Watched orderlies take you from your room,
Put you in a van, take you to a final resting place
Where you were bathed, called honey and sweetie,
Until the night nurse called your daughter at 1 am and said
Dear, your mother has passed.

ANNA EGAN SMUCKER

Body Shop

Through the window, above the sign
Danger/Stay out, I watch the workers
consulting, poking at the innards of cars
and trucks jacked up over their heads.

In the tire-and-cigarette scented
waiting room, Fox News drones on.
No, the others would not prefer
changing to the Weather Channel.
I breathe in, breathe out,
but that doesn't last.
I'm tired.
I want out of here.

After six hours, four of us
remain. We've drunk car-shop coffee,
eaten all the Cheez-Its, Nabisco Pretzels,
and Chips-A-Hoy Minis. And we talk:

the tattooed woman with piercings
and purple hair tells of her partner
who overdosed last week,
wishes she'd been a better listener.

The elderly woman, who looks like
Coretta Scott King, had a narrow escape
on foggy I-68. Twisting a Kleenex
she watches the snow beginning to stick.

In a voice that rattles in his chest,
the man says he should've known
thirty years underground would get him
silicosis and a heart winding down.

I look at these weary people on these God-awful
plastic chairs and give thanks for the steady rhythm
of *my* heart, and suddenly I see *their* hearts,
really see them—beating, glowing, pulsing;
all vulnerable. All the same.

MARCIA SHUBERT

Every Little Thing

STEPHANIE KENDRICK

Dragging my Heart around Appalachia

Crossing the Ohio River smells like wet iron
and catfish until you hit Kentucky, and Goldenrod
and fried chicken smacks your face so hard
tears fly out of your eyes.

Tennessee wind swirls
through your ears a low moan,
carrying with it the sound of Aretha, soul
swelling air that makes your hips shift
without asking permission.

When you walk the sands of the Carolinas,
your right hand can't stop grasping
the air by your hip, for one that waved goodbye
years ago and left
salt-water scars on your cheeks.

The accent picked up in Georgia
drips down your chin like peach spit
when you remember the woman at the truck stop
with the bloodshot eyes who worked so hard
to upsell you cherry pie.

Isn't the ruffed grouse insane?
To stay in Pennsylvania all year, never flying south
as though it loves the snow,
or dare I say, its home.

Maryland cigarettes burned to ash,
and by the time the gas ran out in Alabama
you were sucking old filters,
making up curse words, your mother
flying out of your mouth in bursts of smoke.

You try to remember Mississippi, but you can't.
Beer in hand as soon as you crossed that border
as if you'd been running on fumes, too.

Every time you cross state lines,
you hold your breath.
The smell of sour mash or dandelion stems
tickle your nose,
a warm breeze whispers in your ear-
now, you're home.

Stephanie Kendrick

To the Women of Appalachia

       hustlers of the hills and valleys
and every mountain top in between.
       To women who defy laws of time
and space,
       because we have shit to do.
Women who one day cradle cooing baby,
       and the next day wave them off to war.
Women who know that war happens in deserts,
       and in their own backyards. Big Pharma-
modern day coal companies-
       hollowed out our people this time.
To women who spend their summers saving-
       green beans and tomatoes from the garden,
saving money by using the clothesline,
       and saving all the empty-bellied neighbor kids.

To the women of Appalachia,
       mountain mommas who work full time,
take online classes and still
       have dinner on the table.
To women who raise daughters,
       earn their GED,
and order takeout instead.
Women who know Virginia Creeper as a pesky vine,
       and the ones who know it as a strain of pot.
Women who take belly dancing classes
       and still call complete strangers *babydoll*.
Women who leave bread on front porches
of neighbors they will later gossip about
       before adding them to prayer chains.

To the women who take bourbon in their coffee,
and the ones who never touched that stuff,
       because they saw what it did to their mommas.
To their mommas, who just want to forget.
To the women who write poems in their showers,
and refuse to edit the *y'alls* and *hollers*

that inevitably crawl their way in.
To all these women and the women they know,
the roots holding us from being washed away,
the anchors that keep the current from pulling us under,
the stars that guide us home.

Susan E. Powers

The Fall (Song)

Now you're almost grown
How hard it is to be alone
Now you're almost grown
Just what you're thinking never shows
Divides so wide I cannot cross
A thousand waterfalls are not enough

Chorus
They will fall, fall, fall, fall, fall
Till they find someone to shelter
They will fall, fall, fall, fall, fall
Till they find someone

You're almost grown
You've got a mind of your own
Now you're almost grown
And I have a mind to just let go
Feel like you're going to save the child
But they really don't need saving

Chorus

You're almost grown
You want to see what the others see
Now you're almost grown
Don't want to take more than you need
Every single beating heart
Feels a moving part across the water.

Chorus

BARBARA MARIE MINNEY

Country Hill Music

men in faded and tattered coveralls,
    plaid shirts,
sleeves rolled up to the elbows,
women in threadbare gingham dresses
    faces shadowed by the fading light,
    sitting on front porches
        of dilapidated cabins
after a long day struggling in the fields
behind horse drawn plows
    slicing fiddles and banjos
listening to country hill music
    reverberating through the hollows

recognition hovering like dandelion fluff
    just out of reach
swimming on the whitecaps of the notes

the boy, no longer there,
gingerly holding the neck of a five and dime store guitar,
    crossing the murky creek
    on a bridge of roughhewn logs,
remnants of the spring wash out

sneaking off to look at girlie magazines
    hidden under the floor of the old corn crib
choking on cigarettes and moonshine
    behind the barn
picking paw paws and blackberries in the hills
shooting crawdads in the creek
    with a brand-new BB gun
fishing in the pond with bamboo poles and shiny bobbers,
squirrel gravy simmering on the wood stove
    perfume of fresh baked biscuits
        filling the senses
    shivering on the way
through the potato patch
    to the outhouse

where did that boy go?
    life was simpler then
        just harder
you could not lose your soul so easily

    if you listen closely
in the dead of a starless night
grandma's words still echo through the hollows
    "Don't get above your raisin'."

Bonnie Proudfoot

Elegy for Farm Life

Outside the window, peach trees line the field,
the road snakes downhill, then drops
out of sight beyond the ridgeline, west,
toward the setting sun. Chickens roost

for the night, a few yards into the woods, a sow
and piglets root and grunt. Light stripes
the yard in long diagonals, seeps
across the window sill. Watch the girl

at the kitchen window, she raises children,
keeps them safe, plants a garden,
wills it to grow, yanks out the weeds.
Watch her read The Joy of Cooking,

check how to sterilize jars for canning,
see diagrams of the cuts of meat
note the correct internal temperature.
The yearling pig looks her in the eyes

before they shoot it. Is that how
it is supposed to work? Yes, others
have been here before, they knew
what to do, she thinks she has something

she needs to prove. Chickens come racing over,
follow even to the slaughter. Each time,
the eyes dull, the distance is less than
a weightless breath. Heat stays in the warm flesh.

She used to think that she could do anything,
that she could be anyone she willed herself
to be. It was a story she told herself,
as if the telling could make it true.

Blood stains the ground dark brown.
She walks past the chopping block, the meat saw.
The house smells like death. The work

is not done until it is done. She knows that.

Look, here are photos, peach trees in bloom,
the setting sun that streams across the yard.
There she is at the window, holding on for dear life,
the light so bright, the kitchen so clean.

KATHERINE ZIFF

Athens Alone Together

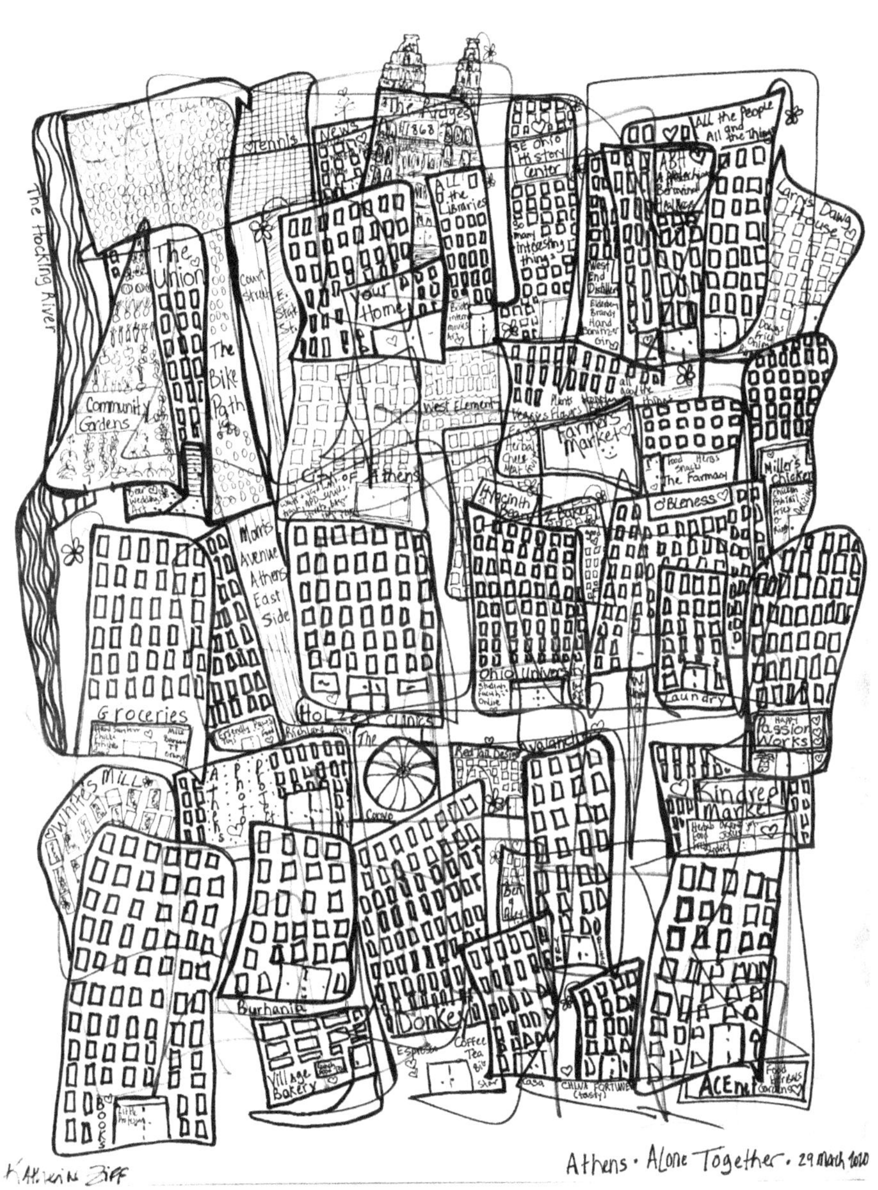

KAtherin Ziff

Athens · Alone Together · 29 March 2020

Pauletta Hansel

Interview

> "Anyone who wishes to write the truth must overcome at least 5 difficulties."
> –Bertolt Brecht

1.

Let's go back to 1975.
Pauletta, you're...
     caught stitched at the seam of the mountain. I felt real trapped.
Times New Roman, you're...
     a loose thread,
leaving and coming back...
     The truth is it was a lot looser than that.
Go on.
     The truth is my life has been a constant moving between.
Let's go back...
     Over time things mend and it's not as if you can't see the cracks.
to 1975.
     People were beginning to believe
     they could do something about the powers that had affected them all
     their lives.
So lead me through some lives here.
     They were looking to their history.
     The pressures from the outside were kindling a strength
Let's go back ...
     to find a place where people have a voice,
     where they never had one before.
to 1975.
     The truth is what we saw wasn't really there.
     There are other ways to measure. The truth
Pauletta,
     is I think it took me longer to find what didn't fit.
     As it was, what I chose to do was to leave and to stay gone.
you're 15.
     The truth is I haven't written in that way for many years.

2.

You are trying to remember what trapped meant to you then. The mountains pushing in, and how the only voice you had was typed on the page. You lived two lives. The mirror cracked, and you somewhere outside it, watching. Remember? You couldn't pass a glass without looking for your own reflection, see your hand move up to touch your own mouth.   *Shh.*   What? W h a t did you want to tell me? There is the history on the typed page. You were a girl who wrote yourself into a woman. There is the history of the body. ***Shhh! We don't talk. We don't talk about...*** Remember? His hand pushing down your head your mouth to where it was made you a woman. You are trying to remember trapped, the girl you want to strip away, the soft slough of her useless to you now, the woman all hard planes, a hundred shattered shards hold girl, behind her, mountains all around and pushing. There is a road, but the road is still inside you. For all your black typed words trapped on the page, you have not found it yet. You are trying. Remember.

3.

```
reading womanpoems,
my fingers
reach wildly.
paper!
pen!
underneath the nails,
i feel them,
womanlines,
screaming
for release.
quick!
before i
bite them away.
                p.h.
```

You were 15 when you wrote that poem/when i wrote this poem, i was 15

I haven't written in that way for many years.

4.

Let's go back, but not all the way back.

5.

15 years after I was 15, I was interviewed about being an Appalachian poet,
which I wasn't anymore. Not then.
A poet, I mean.
>
> *Let's go back*
>
> *to 1975.*
>
> *Pauletta, you're…*

The year before I turned 15, I had sex with a man ten years older.
>   (Call it what it was)

Being already a poet, I told it slant,
>   (You were raped)

the angle of the mirror cocked
>   (***i called it making love***)

so even my eye
could not catch the *i*
of the girl
>   (***i called myself a woman***)

I wanted not to be.

Over the years, I wrote myself
out of that girl and into silence.

        I haven't written in that way for many years.

I am trying to write her voice back into me.
I am looking to my history.
I am kindling a strength.

        It's not as if you can't see the cracks.

Kristi Stephens Walker

Carrot cake

Carrot cake comes after, never during.
The meal, the bread, even the wine, are all just
foreplay for the eventual satisfaction of a tastiness
that began when a long, hard root vegetable was plucked, ripe, from the ground.

Ready to eat cakey flesh and nuts, baked until they rise to the occasion.
Hard, moist, trembling slightly, the bounce of a nipple-hard breast,
back arched and nerves on fire when the baker flips it over,
a free fall from cake pan to cake plate.
Divided, right down the middle by a creamy dollop of real whipped cream,
that whole cake just ready to be eaten.
Carrot cake was meant to be shared, and slid across the table,
the last bite savored, swallowed, tasted to the last pleasure.
A sweetness—not saccharine but sacrament—warm between the folds.

Kristi Stephens Walker

How To Peel A Peach

That wickedly warm July day, we brought home peaches from the stand and
I said I would teach you how to peel a peach without bruising it.
We would, I said to you while you were already behind me, unbuttoning my
    oxford,
make a cobbler.
You covered my hands with yours,
following along as I pierced the knife to quarter that succulent Georgia peach,
fuzzy, and the ripest one of the bunch.
The pieces fell right off the pit and in one single motion, I peeled back the skin
offering you a bite.
The peach juice ran down your chin and I kissed it off your lips,
the kitchen filling with the scent of fecund passion and Petrichor
when the clouds broke and, finally, rain poured outside.

The cobbler never got made, and for three days, neither did the bed.

What did we think would happen to three bushels of peaches?
You didn't know how to get at what was inside without wounding the flesh
    around it.
You waited too long to enjoy the mesocarp, always thinking you would get to it
    eventually.
Everything has a shelf life.

Danielle Byington

Athena Waters Her Flowers

KAREN WHITTINGTON NELSON

Motherless Girls

Like baby birds
left unattended,
motherless girls
huddle hungry,
shiver in the cold,
naked but for
downy vulnerability &
the itch of pin feathers.

Motherless girls,
like abandoned
baby birds,
trill, "Love me!"
as they scratch for
tidbits of affection
beneath layers of neglect,
dig until their raw feet
hit rejection.

Left to wither,
motherless girls &
forgotten birdlings
withdraw deeper into
twist & tangle,
fall silent & spent,
too weak to chirp.

The most desperate
or daring plunge
over the rim of the world
into the void. Some fall into
gaping jaws, shatter on impact,
or ache for the belonging songs
that they were never taught.
The lucky ones,
like my mother & her sisters,
jump holding hands,
the buoyancy of their bond
holding them aloft.

Karen Whittington Nelson

Homecoming

He busies his impatient hands,
adjusts himself, checks his zipper,
creases the seam of his trousers,
waits for his daughter
in this parked car
that has carried him
the distance

up river,
a hundred or so miles
as the crow flies—
to this place along the Muskingum
where his daughter
chooses to smother her own light,
to hide inside a room
locked from the outside,
protected by her own craziness
from his.

He waits, anticipating the
timid, chemical shuffle across
the graveled parking lot, her
quiet-before-the-storm approach.
He's missed her, can't wait to see her.
His girl.

Thoughts roll through his head
like sooty smoke seeking a crack
through which to escape and muddy the sky:
the abandoned rest stop at the edge of town,
the car concealed in a copse of neglected pines,
the unexpected force it takes to hold her
frail body splayed across the backseat—
A tap on the window derails his thoughts,
a figure in scrubs stutters an apology,
mumbles condolences.

He will not be fetching his daughter today. She
could not wait for him, has already left.
Please, let her mother know, her beloved girl
will be along soon, expected to surface down river
close to her mama's house in but a few days, or so.

72

S. Renay Sanders

Quillin'

"Nace, you ever heard of quillin'?" my Uncle Hamp asked me from across his kitchen table. "No, I don't believe I have," I responded, while wondering to myself what tall tale he was fixing to tell. Uncle Hamp dabbed at the perspiration on his brow, leaned back in his rickety chair and said, "Well then, let me tell you. This is something your Uncle Randall was a-talkin' about the other day."

At this point I should explain in addition to storytellers my uncles were farmers, occasional moonshiners, and often worked outside of the farm to make ends meet. Uncle Randall worked in maintenance for the Grundy County school district in central Tennessee. One day he was out on the mountain at the high school coaxing an old air conditioner back to life. He got to talking with one of the lunch ladies about the old days. Randall told how his mama had been a midwife. The woman said then you must know about quillin'. But Randall didn't reckon he did.

"Well," she began, "let me tell you this story my mama used to tell from back in the day." Back then people didn't fool much with doctors and hospitals—especially not for having babies. Randall agreed with this, knowing that was true from growing up with a midwifing mama. Doctors were scarce in rural Tennessee. Back then they were generally not seen as needed to attend births as farm people knew how to birth things. It was a part of life, an everyday miracle of sorts. Going to a hospital just to have a baby was all but unheard of as midwives made house calls.

She told Randall of one time when the local midwife had been called to tend to a woman, a girl really, about to have her first baby. They'd been at it all night and still had no baby. Finally, the anxious father-to-be decided to go get the doctor, leaving his young bride and the midwife behind.

The midwife had done everything she knew to do except one thing, which she was hesitant to try alone. Meanwhile, the young woman continued to labor. The daddy returned with Doc Hollins in tow. Doc set in to do his exam and asked the midwife about how things had gone through the night. The midwife told how the labor went on and on even though they had tried all different positions to get that baby moving, but nothing, no baby.

She said, "I got the mama up to walk around but still, no baby. The pains were a coming regular but they would stop and then start again." Doc reached into his bag and produced a stethoscope.

"This girl is just about tuckered out Doc," the midwife said as worry washed over her face. "She's a-scared. I don't know how much longer she can last."

Thankfully, the doctor heard a good strong heartbeat from the baby so he wasn't too worried. Not yet anyway. He did some massaging of mama's belly and determined the baby was in a good position to be born. But still no matter how hard and long the young mama pushed, that baby was not coming out. With exasperation, the midwife turned to Doc and said, "Do you think we oughta quill her?"

Quill her? The doctor had no idea what that was, but being new to these parts and fairly young, he wasn't about to let on that he didn't know. "No, no, not yet," he stammered, shifting in his seat.

The labor continued, but still no baby. The old lady once again asked if it was time to quill her. In desperation, Doc finally agreed even though he still had no idea what was about to happen. He just nodded to the midwife and sighed, "Get it ready."

The old lady took up a cast iron skillet and put it on the wood stove where she'd been boiling water. She got that skillet just a burnin' hot.

"Get ready Doc!" she hollered. In a flash she grabbed the skillet, threw some black pepper on it, and stuck the whole thing up under that poor girl's nose.

"Take a deep breath, little Mama," said the midwife.

Little mama did and she let out a sneeze that echoed throughout the cove and plum up the mountain and out popped that youngin's little head into the waiting hands of Doc Hollins.

Uncle Hamp crossed his arms and quietly chuckled to himself as he recounted the tale. I helped myself to another glass of tea and he continued to talk.

"Now, you know once we found out about quillin', me and Randall was just a dying to try it but didn't know when we were apt to get a chance. But don't you know it wouldn't be but about a week when your own cousin Bonnie Lee brought her littlest boy, Bow Pete, up here to the house. She was almost in tears."

"This youngin has stuck a bean way up in his nose," she cried, "and I can't get it out!" I turned and looked at Randall across the room and we just nodded to each other. "Randall! Get the skillet!" I said. It was time for a quillin'. When that pepper hit that hot skillet Bow Pete let out such a sneeze that it echoed throughout the cove and plum up the mountain and not one *but two* beans came flying out of that boy's nose.

"And *that*, Nace, is what you call a quillin,'" Hamp said with a satisfied grin. "You just never know when it might come in handy."

Epilogue:

A Google search revealed that quilling was indeed an established birthing technique. The original method was to put pepper on the end of a goose quill which was stuck in mother's nostril causing her to sneeze and the baby to be born. I found no evidence of when the switch was made to the frying pan.

KARI GUNTER-SEYMOUR

Sisters From Another Mother

Jennifer Hambrick

Spitting Downstairs

Third floor, Ishmael Apartments
no elevator even on grocery days –
I'm seven years old and outside
grandmother's door looking down
over the dark wood bannister and I spit
straight down into its spiral echo
around and around each flight of stairs
all the way down to the ground floor
all the way through black grouting
between white hexagonal tiles
old, like worn-out chicken wire
to the barnyard and great-grandmother
wringing supper's neck, waiting
for supper to stop flailing
reflexively flapping, waiting for supper
to go silent. Spit splats a cold smack
like limp flesh on hard white countertop
the only sound in the silence
of the barnyard stunned cluckless
as though every voice in solidarity
with the one squeezed out with the neck
that held it tight, along with the one
that longed for the length
and breadth of the world beyond
barnyard, beyond cast iron skillet
beyond chicken wire and porcelain tile
beyond bannister, beyond sagging
apartment, beyond the desperate silence
of failed freedom, just beyond.

Jennifer Hambrick

The Rib of Eve

The story goes
that in the garden
Adam sacrificed a rib,
not knowing that Eve
would come of it,
that he gave her his flesh,
the viper's nest
that would spell their end.
I am told
that when she stood on the land
that bore her mothers,
my great grandmother
resembled from a distance
a diagonal line
leaning toward the right,
winds stirring bluegrass at her feet,
as she pressed her fist into the pain
that lived in her left side
just below the ribs.
I'm told she always stepped farther
with the right leg than with the left,
as though to flee the pain
that now catches at my waist
and steals my breath.
I wonder if Adam
walked around the garden
with his hand on his side,
pressing into the wound
to stanch the ache
that flowed to Eve
and all the generations.
Or maybe this was Eve's job,
to clutch her penance
for damning her children
forever.

Karen Scott

The Guitar Player's Wife

He wooed me with his music
Strumming and singing on my Daddy's porch
perched on the West Virginia hillside.
I fell in love with the music
then I fell in love with the man.

Now this is my life
sitting in bars, pizza parlors and festivals
in Ohio, Kentucky and home.
This is how I spend my weekends
as we go from town to town.

I glare at inconsiderate people
talking loudly on their phones
or college kids partying,
drowning out my husband as he sings.

I make myself invisible
so people will concentrate on him
who wooed me with his voice and song
'til I fell in love with the man.

I sway and tap my foot.
Sometimes I sing along
as people fall in love with his music
and I keep loving the man.

KAREN SCOTT

I Used To Think I was A Southerner Until Kari Told Me Otherwise

I never thought of myself as Appalachian, you know, because I'm black?
Even though I am tactful to a fault, love pecans, peaches, pralines,
and covet wraparound verandas and sleeping porches,
I guess I'm not a Southerner.

When I think of Appalachia, I think of houses we worked on as teens
during a Protestant Youth of the Chapel mission trip.
We stayed in dorms at Berea College at night, dispersed throughout the
community during the day to paint and do minor repair.
I remember drinking the best tasting water from a well, pulled up in a metal
cylinder on a chain or delivered from a hand pump after a lot of priming!

I grew up acknowledging only North and South of the Mason Dixon Line.
My roots are probably MidAtlantic, though. It was believed that Granddaddy
Ernest Mills got his surname from the Yancey Mills near Richmond, VA.
Grandaddy Cleve was able to pass, was a shopkeeper in Boissevain.
I recently found the whole Wilkins family listed as *white* on the 1940 census!

When I think of Appalachia, I think of small homes perched on a hillside
Tarpaper shacks set next to the road and porches without railings.
Unpainted, weathered wood. The dusty roads of the 50s and 60s
The sights I would see on the way to visit relatives
in Chatteroy and Pocahontas in the summers.

Come to think of it, we never traveled to visit relatives in Mississippi or
Alabama like a lot of black kids did.
We didn't have any relatives there!
All European immigrants did not come through Ellis Island;.
Nor did all enslaved black people arrive through Georgia or the Carolinas. A
lot entered through Maryland and Virginia, migrated north and west from
there.

But we're black, so we must be Southern, right?
Frank X. Walker to the rescue!
Coining the term *Affrilachian*, defining, reminding us that Appalachia has
always been diverse. The world just needed to be *woke*.

Karen Scott

A Mouthful of Idiom and Colloquialism

How do you say Appalachian? If you are from the Southern Appalachians then you, without a doubt, say Appa-LATCH-uh. If you say Appa-LAY-shuh you are not only identifying the mountain range but you are also announcing to all that you are not from there. You can say a lot in just one word. From: *https:// coalfieldstocornfields.wordpress.com/*

I know of tipples and denuded mountaintops and the difference between
anthracite and bituminous coal. I know the lines in rock created by blasting
caps and bridges over deep ditches, the reason for saying
The good Lord willin' and the creek don't rise.

I've driven narrow highways where one ROUGH ROAD sign covered the
next 20 miles. Gone around hairpin curves where I swear
I could almost see my rear license plate in the side mirror!
I know the snaky road sign, where each turn takes you into the neighboring
state. Back and forth, a serpentine highway, ending in a town divided.
Watching for FALLING ROCK and unexpected obstacles just around the
bend.

I don't think skunks ACTUALLY get drunk and I don't know
who Cootie Brown is or why he and a polecat might share their inebriation!
I don't know who Dick is or why he wears his hat so tight!

I HAVE seen the Dairy Queen where my mother and father went on dates,
climbed the steps on the Bluefield State campus where they met.
I've eaten at the Lock, Stock and Barrel Restaurant in Bluefield,
stayed in The Mountaineer Hotel in Williamson,
shopped at the Piggly Wiggly near Pikeville, Kentucky and
bought a dress at the Peebles too.

I can clean the soot from the chimney of a kerosene lamp, fill it and trim the
wick. I have done laundry with a wringer washer and even a washboard and
tub. Hanging the clothes on a line to dry, wooden clothespins stuck in my
mouth.   I know how a dusty road up the holler can coat your patent
leather shoes. You better change into your play clothes right away unless you
want your Momma to have a hissy fit!

I know how old the Bible says Methuselah was, but I am not as certain about
the age of dirt. I know how long dogs and cats usually live
but I'm not really sure how many years are in a coon's age.
I know Vaseline is good for getting rid of ashiness but I hate how it smells
If you asked my Granddaddy how he was, he would tell you
Fine and dandy like Hershey candy!
I was raised on *Pretty is as pretty does,* warned by Daddy that *there's no need
to buy the cow when you can get the milk for free.*
I was told to *let your conscious be your guide. It's better to give than to
receive.*   I often heard *if it had been a snake, it woulda bit you*
and Momma was often *fit to be tied.*

She'd say *Beggars can't be choosers.* If I wanted some of what she didn't
want to share, I would hear - *Your eyes may water. Your teeth may grit.
But none of this are you gonna git.*

I still ask for an ink pen and for tin foil, put food in the icebox
and claim my brother *has always been a little touched in the head.*

Momma would tell me that *People in hell want ice water too*
Remind me to *mind my p's and q's a*nd always *Practice what you preach.*
And now that I am *getting on in years,* I find I've got more aches than
Carter's got Little Pills. But *it beats a poke in the eye with a sharp stick!*

So when I'm *runnin around like a chicken with its head cut off*
Can't make heads nor tails of it, confused as *all get out*
I remember another thing Granddaddy would say,
From a rock in the cradle to a roll in the hearse
There's nothing so bad that it couldn't be worse.

And I smile.

Sylvia Freeman

Kin

SARA MINGES

Sunday Paper, Disgruntled Salesman, and a Dollar and Thirty Five Cents

Lazily curled up in
lavender-smelling sheets,
naked bits peeking out
here and there
awoken from her slumber
by glimpses of sun and her
pounding headache,
remnants of last night's
frat party

Dry mouth reminds her she
needs a cup-o-java,
perhaps it will make her
hangover go away,
she hopes.

Clad in her favorite jeans,
she grabs the T-shirt
hanging on the chair.

Flip-flops, oversized designer glasses,
pulls her long locks into a loose ponytail.

Headed down the Tennessee hill to the
gas station
for coffee, funnies, and the
Sunday news

Ex-marine stands alert at the counter, frowning.
She hurries over to the newspaper stand,
disappointed to see the top copy crumpled,
likely missing the juicy parts.

Halfway down she pulls out a crisp, fresh copy
A burley voice says, "You need to take the one on the top."

Disclaimer:

Knoxville men often believe women
have no brains and belong in the kitchen,
barefoot and pregnant.

"But sir," (I say in my best
Nebraska girl-turned-Tennessean accent),

"Your top paper is all crumpled.
I want to make sure I get
all the juicy parts.
I straightened your stack,
all real nice and neat, I used to work retail."
He puffs up, glares and
smacks back a retort,
"Oh, so you think that
dollar and thirty five cents
gives you the right to decide what paper
you get to buy."

Sassy brain kicked in, smiling,
I stared right back and said,
"You're damn right I do."

SUSANNA NESTOR

September 11, 1965

The burgundy corvair was twisted and smoldering in a yard on Dorman Drive. People on that street hire gardeners who aren't kids to mow their lawns. The car was dead earlier that day so I poured coca cola on the battery terminals to get rid of corrosion, hooked up cables, put in fresh oil and aired up the tires. I slapped the hood and told my brother he was good to go. He was going over the hill to Sciotoville to visit a pretty girl named Valerie.

Jim never had much luck with the girls from Portsmouth. He stuttered a lot, always got cut from baseball. His eyes were always shifting back and forth and he counted to himself. No one thought much of it back then; they just called it awkward. He was constantly in trouble with my dad because he didn't know a screwdriver from a wrench. "Don't worry," I always told him. "Sissy knows all the tools and can fix anything for you. We don't have to tell anyone, just pretend you did it."

It was my thirteenth birthday. Giggling girls had just arrived when the call came in. We were having pink and blue decorated cake from the store and pizza delivery. It was the first time I was getting store bought food. The cake had sparkles and squeazy frosting with my name. The pizzas were covered in silver dollar pepperoni. Until then, pizza delivery was something I only had at rich friends' houses. Balloons were everywhere and colored napkins matched the plates. This was a real party like on TV. Other birthdays had always been after church with Grandma and instead of ham or chicken we had a special meal like fish sticks and crinkle French fries. Mom loved German chocolate cake so she always made one. The coconut on it smelled awful. I would ask for different cake but she always just said, "You don't know what's good, stop being picky."

It was just getting dark. He must have been lying there under the canopied maple tree hoping this was a bad dream, slipping in and out of consciousness. Red lights and sirens filled the blackening sky. I hoped he wasn't dead.

I couldn't shake an image of him in that hospital bed as white as can be, eyes now closed, vacant speech, absolute silence. I hoped he wasn't in trouble. Even more, I hoped he wouldn't get yelled at. But he did. Mama and Daddy told him he ruined my birthday party and he "didn't need no girl over the hill, they's plenty of girls right here. And that car isn't gonna fix itself so that's the end of it."

The next day I got to see him. He was black and blue and stuck with tubes. Broken ribs made it hard for him to breathe. He asked me if he was going to die. I convinced him not to worry and he would get fixed. I knew the bones at least would mend. "Sorry about your party," he cried, tearful, his voice weak. I told him that parties are overrated. Jim scooted over, motioned me closer. "Me and Valerie were having so much fun. Don't tell but we got into her daddy's whiskey and were cutting up until her mama told me it was time to leave." I asked if he got any kisses. "Of course. Just a few and she is like a real girlfriend. We had popcorn. She doesn't make fun of me. Now I guess we have to break up."

I wished he hadn't wrecked that car.

I wished for more Valeries.

I wished it wasn't just the bones that broke in him that night.

I wished my tools could have fixed more than dead batteries.

I wished mama and daddy weren't always mad.

I wish normal   didn't have to be so cruel.

I wish there weren't birthdays.

KATHARINE STUDER

Saving the Children

Sidney Ison could see
the locust swarming
the pear trees.
She would chase them
with her long handled
broom, months before the neighbors
could hear their high tenor songs,
believing if paired in groups,
they might mate and mate and never quit,
stripping the leaves and bark to a stick.

She taught them to keep
looking for what cannot be seen.
Somedays she would scribble
a list on the wooden table
her husband Wink made from
the rotten maple that fell
on the roof, just far enough from
the door frame, to save the house.
On her list she would scribble:
  sugar
  tabasco sauce
  cinnamon
  chard to be boiled.
Other days she would sit at the table
drawing lines through the things
she could do without:
  replace tabasco with ground pepper,
  drain the beehives.

On the Sabbath, through hollered complaints
of how church was a waste
of a perfectly good Sunday,
she would spit bath the children's faces with a hankie
as they entered the church doors with
hushed words and absent parents,
telling them to kneel,
to pray, to understand,

they came from the coal mining
soil they carried on their soles,
from the muddy corn fields that ran off the hills
and from those voices that knew how to sing
        Halleluiah, how to keep standing,
        to sing praise.

Kathleen S. Burgess

Sanctuaries

Four walls define us for the duration,
season or seasons, still unknown. We
watch maps as haloed, early life forms
pass through the world, reach every

host, multiply within. If we open up,
viral clouds could enter. The wealthy
extol as virtue that some must *take one*
for the nation's good: *Go back to work.*

Our infections, a small matter to them.
You and I—our work years lie behind us.
Death may cling to hair, fingers, faces,
lungs on a day that begins like any other.

But…. Oh! The mystery of where-when
how: *Not-now-not-now-not-not-today*, I
nightmare. Mourning doves wake before
dawn. Light raises us from bed. Song

sparrows heft and balance twigs, flying
them to their nests. For jonquils, earth
opens innumerable mouths to the rain.
Forsythia, too, flares into fountaining.

Kathleen S. Burgess

Uncertain March
for Jack

By Caldwell Lake, a dry percussion
of leaves leached thin, color faded
as sepia print. Memories whisper of

other seasons. One leaf cartwheels
in. Floats. Sandwiches on our lips
and tongues feel like wood. Finish

as whole-grain bread with cheese,
firm but not so thick in the mouth.
Twig and branch swell with buds.

Maple sap has begun its rise and
fall, sweet in a bald, southern Ohio
winter, unsettling for all who think

of freeze and denial. Spring will
yield uncertain futures; the futures,
to certain ends. Under the high

ever-blue, we cross a red, wooden
footbridge. Below water glistens,
ripples so swiftly from hill to lake

that I wonder how the tide-restless
ocean floors could ever petrify.
Fragments of shell and coral surface

limestone boulders longing above
the channel. In sand, among prints
of raccoon and deer and geese,

adolescents have written *Emily,*
Scott, and a swear with sticks. All
this persists after yesterday's rains.

Kathy Guest

Dream Study

Kathleen S. Burgess

Lines of Disappearance, Chillicothe, Ohio, 2014-2015

In memory of Tameka Lynch, Shasta Himelrick, Timberly Claytor, Tiffany Sayre, Rebecca Cade, and Charlotte Trego and Wanda Lemons, both still missing

The filament, like a trip wire, shivers
        across the trail of one who
waits, as patient as deadly.

        In the shade, a tilt from upright,
a wobble along the axis of a moral universe.

        A hickory tussock caterpillar dangles,
descends. Fragile. On its back a black line
        connects the dots.

Intoxicated by need, she slips away
        from home, to find, to make a new home.

The slender silk escape ruptures. The world,
        seen from ineluctable hunger,
blinds her, as it binds her to danger—

        a foreshortened future. More disappear.
They are not caterpillars.

        Some vanishings widen a thousand, thousand
eyes. Ensnared, one rides drugged. One is shot.
        One fearing water lies bloated on a sandbar.

Beside a road, another casketed in a drainage pipe
        ripens the air with violent death.

The pirate spider mimics the mating call. He
        plucks a deceptive cadence on her silk thread.
Feeds on her credulity. Forages his next meal.

*Our apologies: This poem was originally intended for *Women Speak*, Volume 5

Kathleen S. Burgess

Landscapes of Grief
Winter, 2018

My heart rocks like a johnboat
on the North Fork Creek, now river

drowning parkland, swamping banks,
the muddy crests shot through

with silver light—the veins of Paint—
Scioto—Ohio—Mississippi—

run every -ville/town/city straight
downriver to New Orleans as flush with

mourners as lantana petals with color.
Beside this Ross County trail,

a gray-furred possum, two days gone,
lies in state. No vultures

yet. Too cold for ants
to elegize with mandibles. How gladdened

I am knowing the white-tailed deer
tread quietly. Watchful in small herds.

Not so many as a nightclub. A high school.
Too much spilled vein. Too much

sprayed silver. Much run. Much tears.
Flowers.

*Our apologies: This poem was originally intended for *Women Speak*, Volume 5.

Susan Truxell Sauter

Waiting

used to be living, for my flowered life to begin,
school bus doors to open, school day to end,
waiting to slip out of my father's troubled household,
for the heavy black phone at the stairway nook to ring,
my boyfriend to pick me up, my sixteenth birthday
when best friend would take me for a Learner's Permit,
waiting for the day after graduation
I'd turn out of that town
and into a city, the pulse
of waiting faster
at the land-grant university,
libraries to close, bars to open,
my future husband to walk in.

Dogs and decades later,
I forgot how to wait and wait some more,
slammed-brakes waiting, pacing time
for a decrease in body and soul sickness,
of course, in COVID cases, or for its vaccine,
when I can hug friends, breathe their unmasked air,
for the November election, the chronic wait
for common good,
for decency to prevail.

Tonight, I wait for the comet Neowise,
but also wait for a surprised doe
grazing in the high meadow to move
her black-hooved foot another step
toward me with her speckled fawn
close by. While she ciphers,
I wait for rain, the milkweed leaves
curled in upon themselves,
the droughty grasses
brittle as I am.

High pitch snort, white-tail
underside lifts, her body a-twitch,
the doe sprints while I wait for nightfall.

I've waited for nature's evening to fall
this and other times and honestly, it doesn't.
Lightning bugs rise, night birds sound,
moon ascends, insects whine in the still air.

SUSAN TRUXELL SAUTER

One Last Waltz

I'd lift your blue left foot to my lap, work
my fingers between the toes, move to the soles,
and over-the-rainbow instep. I'd press
onward to give the neglected foot its due.

You'd sit ancient
        in a maroon, wing-backed chair, a housedress
                billowed over the missing breast and Frankenstein scar.

I'd blow my heart out,
as I do anyway, hoping you'll hear me
through the 1962 Bundy flute you
and Grandma bought with money tight
so I could play in *Orchestra*. I'd tell you how I left
sheet music behind, taught myself to play by ear.

I'd tell you goofy jokes, make you laugh,
to hear how your voice sounded yet again.
I'd paint your portrait, causing you to marvel
at your arty youngest daughter.

If you agreed I'd paint your nails, even the ones
on your toes, Fire Engine Red, your favorite lipstick color.
Gazing up at your face, I'd mention I'd read that part in your diary
about being engaged to Homer, your true love, before my father.
I'd ask if the world war ended your plans, the boatswain cutting
you lose in the meantime. I'd ask why you didn't wait
for him, but of course I wouldn't be
asking anything then.

As I combed your hair, I'd gently ask if
you could recount, from start to finish, how
you came to spend time in Tiffin Mental Hospital,
what they did to you there, if
it helped after losing the stillborn baby boy, if
it helped you return to a household of blame.

Soon we'd smell a cake baking, hear
the screen door screech open. Teacher-friends,
sorority-sisters and even Grandma herself
would bustle in loaded with gifts
to lay at your now-manicured feet.

Later when all was quiet and your cells
pulsed round and pink again, I'd say "Mother, remember
when we used to waltz to *Lawrence Welk?*" You'd nod,
rise, turn on the television console, and with outstretched
hands, take mine in yours.

Wendy McVicker

Orange

Orange, in the palm
of my hand: scented globe,
one splash of color
on a gray day.

Rain coming.

Out walking, we saw
red-orange poppies
crinkled like crepe paper
decorations — but,
no prom this year.

In California, while you
were dying, also in the month
of April, I walked the dog
and collected fallen oranges
that had rolled past the sidewalk
into the grass. Once there,
they were fair game.

They made delicious juice,
nothing like the thin stuff
we drink in Ohio. You smiled,
though I'm not sure you could taste
sweetness by then: so many chemicals
had burned your senses.

This orange has traveled far
to get here. Many hands
have touched it, passing it along
from sunny fields to this gray
morning in Ohio.

I think of all the hands
that have reached out to feed us,
to be fed.

All the hands we cannot touch
during a pandemic.

I cradle this orange in my palm,
smooth and round: the sun
on a cloudy day, a kind
of promise

Beth Jane Toren

Clean Coal Crik Doggerel,
or, Foggy Mountain Nervous Breakdown

Exposed industries
Work
As therapy
      The dull destruction
of the surface mine
cub embryos mummify coiled
overburden
excess rock and soil
laden with toxic mining byproducts
seal the entrance of would be mother bear's den
poisonous runoff sinks to the sulfur orange bed of the shallow new crik
the old crik filled with holler fill and slag
1979 Seneca Rocks Campground
lifting my beer to the galaxy
I hollered
Here's to the dead miners!
"Coal mine safety laws written in miners' blood"
It's 2018
Long live the dead miners!
Rest on a moss covered boulder among the rhododendrons
Look up at the night
Black as a coal miner's coffee when young
For the old's black as his lung
Watch a child god take white chalk to the sky
Connecting the dots
Constellations:
      Dead opossum
 Tire on fire
      Rusted out washing machine in a creek (a beheaded dog floats by)
      One remaining tooth
      Crawdad
My spine and body curvy as 2 $^{1/2}$ hours of narrow harrowing switchback
doglegged mountain roads to get where the crow flies in – he's already there
and back – to arrive 50 years ago at my mineshaft nightmare
In a moment
I'll turn the spotlight on
and see myself
deer in headlights

Blood
Red as a cardinal
flows from her chest
Hold me under crooked back creek
Finite numb
Buried beneath mud
Beneath Queen Anne's lace
Once a mountain woman of constant sorrow
attending Too Tall's dance

Out flat snake road
Rotten hog hill
White opossums faces
Stare down from dark branches
Hollows dark as coal
in an underground mine

Shadow dancers
Spinning dervishes
light fuses at each turn
an old oil barrel
farm
White Lightning

Juggalo tribe
Elders
courteously thank tonight's sponsors:
Dance by OxyContin
Fire by gasoline
Screams by powerless rage

Eyes dried open by Cheap trucker speed
breaking 18 laws
Moses and Nimrod too stupid to stay off the road?
Run em down
like a hollow with a washed out footbridge

Give thy neighbor
Venison baloney
Washed down with the three legged dog of beers
gentle soft spoken natures
belied by thundering desperation

Jessica Weyer Bentley

Birchie

I see her now in my childhood mind; the four dank rooms she
shuffled through; oxygen tank and cracked hands—the Lucky Strikes
had done their work.

She had an odd way about her as she sat on her little couch; a coffee
table near filled with ashtrays, crochet and quilt patterns.

She rocked slightly as if rocking her infant; maybe a habit she could not
cast away. She had rocked thirteen babies since she herself
was thirteen.

A mother's way of holding on a little longer to the
preciousness of being needed.

Her children are grown and a few had slipped away, but on Sunday
her house was filled with their memories. There were murmurings of their
children, their work in the mines or simply laughter to pass the
molasses that was Appalachian time.

As they filed in she would scutter about the kitchen creating her
masterpiece from pinto beans, lard, and flour. No one was allowed to
cook but her—everyone washed their dish to show respect of their
full bellies and quieted hearts.

For someone with meager means she fed us all—Jesus breaking
bread. Instead hers was cornbread and blackberry dumplings.

On summer nights as a thunderstorm graced the sky, Birchie and I
would swing on her front porch where laughter would turn to
conversation and lessons on life.

We would retire to bed falling asleep to Rockford Files and her muffled
snoring.

Birchie, she was not boring; a .22 under her pillow and a daily billow
of smoke about her living room ceiling.

Her cough ever present as she painted her fingernails red, crocheting
blankets and stitching quilts for the holidays ahead.

She was a constant for me though the rooms changed a bit from the
four rooms to a hospital bed. We continued our nightly routine
there too, though we watched Johnny Carson instead.

At night I would sleep in the orange chair next to her bed with the
dread of leaving. We would never swing again watching
the rain, but I knew to relieve her from the strain meant I would be
broken.

It broke too; my heart so big for her.

With her last request, her nails were painted pink to match her jogging suit.

Tere Sager

Anne

Lois Spencer

The Initiate

The summer Carrie and I were eleven, she decided to become my friend, and at first that made no sense at all. Naïve and bookish, I played by the rules and loved the smells of mimeographed papers and chalk dust. Street smart and defiant, Carrie was passed on every year because teachers did well to tolerate her for one term. Then it became evident that Carrie's motive when it came to friendship was simple: She loved nothing so much as a patsy. And I was the ideal candidate.

Joining her exclusive circle came with directives. The first time I used the bathroom at her house she went with me and said that shorts and panties had to go down to the ankles. I soundly objected to exposing what I considered private property. Margie, her protégé, was there for back-up, so I complied, knowing Mom would go through the roof if she found out.

Initiates also had to help Carrie babysit. Young mothers desperate for freedom entrusted their babies and toddlers to Carrie for hours, sometimes all day; Margie and I served as unpaid assistants for onerous jobs like changing soiled diapers. Carrie claimed to know everything about babies, but her foremost area of expertise was how babies were made in the first place. My mom's sketchy information had left a few holes, I found out, which Carrie filled in, expressing shock that anybody my age could be so ignorant. What I wondered was how she knew so much.

A few days into the friendship, I found out that Carrie had sticky fingers. Bold as brass, she snitched two dollars out of the money jar I kept on my dresser with me right there in the room. That afternoon while I bought snacks in the variety store, she further demonstrated her skill by shoplifting a candy bar.

"You almost got caught," I hissed as we left the store. Unruffled, she opened the candy wrapper and offered me half. "No thanks," I said.

She took an exaggerated bite and savored the gooey chocolate. Then she grabbed the bag of snacks out of my hand and trotted down the sidewalk, swinging the bag at her side. I stood in the bright June sunshine and totaled my losses for the day. It was time to take a break.

For two days, I managed to steer clear of her. Then she showed up at my door with Margie. Before I knew what was happening, a scarf covered my eyes and she and Margie were pulling me up the street. The ding of a gas pump signaled the filling station. The close-up smell of diesel and the hiss of air brakes meant we were passing the bus station. But the purr of power mowers and the whoosh of cars were familiar sounds on any street and I lost my bearings.

"If you want loose, tell me where you are," Carrie taunted. I said nothing, so she and Margie spun me around until I was dizzy. When they began leading me again, I realized we were going downhill. The rush of water and hum of tires on grating were unmistakable. I tore my arms free of my captors and threw the blindfold on the ground. Overhead was the bridge crossing the Muskingum River, and we were just feet from the frothing waters of the dam.

* * *

Mom did not approve of my new friendship. Mrs. Carter, she said, was coarse. She swore loud enough to be heard across the street and went outside in a flimsy housecoat and high-heeled mules. And since she worked in a factory, her daughter had an unreasonable number of chores. Even worse, she was left to her own devices. At this point in the narrative, my own thoughts interjected: *Mom, you have no idea.* She reminded me that Mr. Carter was rumored a letch and I was to give him a wide berth. Every Saturday night, the Carters stayed out late drinking and who knew what. They slept it off on Sunday.

As wary as I was after my last encounter with Carrie, I finally let Margie talk me into giving her one more chance. It was Saturday evening, and my parents were sitting on the back porch. I knew they wouldn't abandon *The Saturday Evening Post* or the *Times Recorder* until it was too dark to see the print, and I planned to be home before they had a chance to miss me.

Margie and I found Carrie clearing up from supper and Mr. Carter smoking a cigarette at the table. He seemed to ignore our presence, but it didn't take me long to figure out that he was glancing at the sports page now and then to cover his scrutiny of Margie's smooth white legs. Without being told, Margie filled the sink and began washing dishes. Carrie tossed me a dish towel and started rummaging in a cupboard. Mrs. Carter appeared wearing a dress that left little to the imagination.

"You look pretty, Mommy," Carrie said, opening a box of Little Debbie snack cakes.

"Thank you, baby," Mrs. Carter responded, running her fingers through damp curls. She shook a cigarette out of her husband's pack, lit it with his butane lighter, and inhaled deeply before listing chores Carrie was to do while they were out: mop the kitchen, scrub the bathroom, and vacuum the living room carpet. Carrie groaned. "Mom!"

"Just wait until you grow up," Mrs. Carter countered. "Then you'll learn about real work."

The perfect come-back popped into my head and simultaneously came blurting out of my mouth: "Maybe she'll have a daughter to do her work for her."

Mrs. Carter whirled on a spike heel to face me. This was my cue to apologize, but I was too dumbstruck to oblige. Without comment, she walked to the door and went out, showing a level of discretion Mom would never have believed. Mr. Carter put down his newspaper and adjusted himself as he rose. Seconds later, their car started, breaking the silence. A wicked grin of approbation spread across Carrie's face: Miss Goody-Goody had finally showed some attitude.

Carrie opened the box of snack cakes and shook them onto the table. She gestured Margie and me over. As Margie reached for one, Carrie shook her head. "No shirt at the table." Obediently, Margie pulled off her tee shirt and hunched over as she tore open the package, unable to hide the hard pink nipples and the soft mounds emerging beneath. Carrie looked up at me, waiting, but I remained as I was. "You can keep yours on," she said.

So I was to get a reward. I could eat a chocolate snack cake with my shirt on because I had made a rude remark to somebody's mother. Instead of joining Carrie and Margie at the table, I walked into the peaceful summer evening and waited at the edge of the street for a string of cars to pass. Then I crossed to the other side.

Back home, I grabbed the library book I'd put down when Carrie's lackey had appeared, and Mom scooted over to make room for me in the swing. On the lattice beside us, today's morning glory blossoms had withered, but bright new faces would open in the morning.

* * *

Carrie came to my house the next afternoon as if nothing had changed, and maybe for her it hadn't. She headed straight for my bedroom where I met her in the doorway. "It's not there anymore," I said. Her eyes scanned the dresser top. My trinket box and picture frames, brush and comb and hand mirror were all in their places—everything except the money jar. Then she looked at me as if seeing me for the first time. And maybe she was.

The impact of a small silent figure, stripped of brashness and swagger and returning to her side of the street, has never left me. Nor has contemplating what secret darkness had made her so desperate.

Mary Ann Honaker

When Peeled Back

Beneath morning Folgers, hazelnut creamer,
beneath wet handprints of fog lifting slowly from the window,
beneath thick-inked newspaper and glossy ads rolled into it,

Beneath the smudge of newsprint on your forefinger as your heartbeat
drops another octave, as all the fucks you could give drain from you
more slowly than floodwater drains to lowlands, to ditches,

Beneath the archaic metal dragon unfolding its thin tendons
over the parking lot of smashed Biggie cups and tumbleweed napkins,
all of its teeth filled in, jagged, askew, with bedewed shopping carts,

Beneath neon codes of signs and symbols of every chain restaurant,
store, coffeeshop, the same everywhere beckoning you to the same flavors,
beneath the crushed liquor store box the dread-headed homeless woman sits on,

Beneath the coin you do or do not drop into her strangely fresh, white paper cup,
beneath words you speak flatly over and over again at work, because it's a script
and you cannot, must not deviate, because they are always listening,

Beneath the momentary joy of finding sugar-skull themed coasters,
beneath the low frequency satisfaction of setting them out on your endtables,
and how quickly that glow, like drunkenness, is replaced by a hollow ringing,

Beneath getting everything you want and finding yourself still unhappy,
beneath making a new list to tick off and fall off the cliff of,
beneath how the bones of your city are starting to show, siding in the sideyard,

rafters bare now that the skin of roof has peeled off or has fallen in
like the cheeks of a young woman's body as it mummifies on some remote hillside,
beneath the bruises on a child's arm, the circular stains in the crease of a father's elbow,

Beneath it all when peeled back you find the cruel face of some fey spirit,
whose plump pink hands rub together all the smooth stones of your riverbed:
a god guileless, feral, who smirks at you from under the skin of the world.

MARY ANN HONAKER

Trigger

It's the week after El Paso
and Dayton, Ohio. The grandsons
are here for a visit and my mother

has bought them new Nerf guns.
I'm not judging here--two Christmases
ago I bought them semi-automatic

Nerfs that could fire thirty to fifty
soft foam rounds in one great blaze.
My brother's house was peppered,

pellets in between couch cushions,
wedged under decorative lamps,
rolled under end tables.

*

When we were kids, we played
the cooler version of Cops and Robbers:
Cops and Drug Dealers.

We had tiny pistols that cracked,
argued over who was now dead,
raced around on bikes

equipped with yellow plastic sirens
bolted tight to the handlebars.
The sirens had three settings:

Police Car, Fire Truck, and *Ambulance.*
We never used *Ambulance;*
we never dreamed of aftermath--

*

but now of course kids do.
Kids young as we were then
have known aftermath as a spill

of red from their own bellies.

*

The middle boy immediately
schooled the younger one
on these more complicated,

more life-like guns.

Soon there was an argument.
The ten-year-old strapped

one gun into a shirt waist-tied,
another down the back of his T-shirt,
and held the third, true child warrior

stance. He crept room to room
targeting the four-year-old,
who cried, *Don't shoot me!*

But you shot me in the face!
the older child tattled. Dad tore
the guns from their hands

but not before
the ten-year-old, seething with fury,
pinged a plastic bullet casing

hard on the hardwood floor.
His cry of *unfair* so loud
we all jumped a little, shocked.

*

Super soakers were the rage
when I was in high school.
There was a summer spate

of super soaker drive-bys,
like real drive-bys except
victims were only surprised, wet,

and sometimes, even, refreshed.

*

After El Paso I refreshed my screen
and watched the death toll rise.
The grandkids-- my nephews--

watch hour upon hour
of safe, silly, violence-free
cartoons. But they know

how to jam a cartridge in,
how to rest the butt on a shoulder,
how to pull the trigger.

Corie Neumayer

Final Snow

V.E. PARFITT

Foolish Hope

I prayed with the foolish hope that
somehow god would intervene,
win me the lottery, make me skinny.
Like one time I prayed that the hot water from the shower
would melt the fat away, just wash it out, along
with all the other shit, into the sewer.
My skin was red raw for hours after that prayer.
But I remained fat as ever, dressed in stretchy pants
and a man's sweatshirt, and went to school.

I prayed once for snow, so deep the buses couldn't get through,
because I couldn't do algebra, x's and y's and axes; and gerunds.
I guess I couldn't do English either.
But the snows, they held off, making me miss a Dr's. appointment
three weeks later, to confirm what the lines on the little stick meant.
That answer I did know.

I prayed, once, that god would make it all go away,
please, just go away
and weeks later -
What is it with God and a three weeks lead time?
Three weeks later, you did,
bled out as I was driving down a busy highway.
Too dangerous to pull over on the shoulder, you seeped into the seat.
I left some of you at a rest stop on I75 and then had to stop again,
and finally said goodbye in my bathroom at home.
Well, not my home, but somebody's.

I prayed once, I would know what you looked like,
black hair or light, him or her
And when you visit me in my dreams, with eyes sometimes brown and
sometimes blue,
sometimes old and sometimes young,
I pray that god
just lets me sleep.

V.E. Parfitt

The beauty she is

She is like a poem.
No - like a small book of poetry - easily read in under an hour.
But don't you dare do that.
No, read her one line, one word at a time.

Savor the taste of her, the taste of the words on your tongue.
Is she sweet? ha!
Taste again - or is she like wine, with an oaky, blackberry bouquet,
and a smoky finish.
Taste again - Citricy, melon, h.e.r.b.a.c.e.o.u.s? HA!

Listen to the sound of her,
soft as church bells, cow bells, the wind -
listen again - the howling, biting, blizzard of wind,
whipping sandpaper grit against the window,
Metal on metal, fingernails on a blackboard.
That's the sound of her.

Look at her - see each.and.every.word.
The dirty words, the biting ones, the mean ones.
See the letters that spell h. a. t. e; that spell f. e. a. r.
See the words that form, soundless, from stretched lips
H.e.l.p. H.e.l.p.m.e - I'm lost.

Smell the air around her, feel what she feels.
Feel the t.i.r.e.d in each line. Feel the ready.to.give.up.
Feel the desperation, feel the l.o.n.g.i.n.g.
The longing to love.

Each line a life time.

Feel the passage of a life not felt, like time that
leaves no mark upon the soul,
no wrinkle on the face.
Each line so tightly wrought, sooo well controlled!
Applaud the control! Applause, please.

Please…

Now, only now, read her like the slender volume of poetry she is:
The sweet, the sad, the funny. The words tripping off your tongue,
No effort (on your part).
The fleeting, and the shadows, and the stars and the moon...

Read her like the beauty she is.
A pit for themselves
                         Siddhartha Gautama

Judges gonna judge
and other people too
They hear a name, a phrase
and they think they know
who you are, how you are
what you are.

Three types of judges, one no better
than the other.
There's the: how many kids? wow what fun!
Was it fun? it must have been so much fun!
kind of judge

And then there's the:
how many kids? wow, just wow.
Didn't your parents have tv back then haha
Is that what they did to keep warm lol
Like rabbits
kind of judge.

And then, finally, there's the: how many kids?
your poor mother.
kind of judge.

That's right, my poor mother.
Anybody ever think about her?
Pregnant or nursing for over 20 years; you read that right.
20 years.

But you know what? it's not for you to know. No, my life
is not for you to know. Or judge.

116

I don't ask about your life, I don't chortle, I don't *presume*.
Our life is not for public consumption, you don't need to know,
none of your business in other words. In other words

leave us alone, leave me alone, with your rolling eyes,
your off-hand remarks, your guffaws, and your sniggers.
Why can't you just leave us alone.

One time the priest came to our house,
brought a box of food.
Said, someone told him we were hungry; that we didn't
have any food.

Lies we said, of course we have food.
We opened the cupboards and they were empty;
even I knew they would be empty and I was only six.
The priest shifted uncomfortably, because we had gathered
around his open trunk; mortified by the empty cupboards,
but demanding, with big eyes, to see what he had in there.

He brought out a box with some cans and a few boxes, a bag of something;
beans or pasta or rice? As he handed it to my brother
he did a mental count:
maybe 9 items in the box, the same number of hungry mouths;
or was it 10? He had the grace to be embarrassed.
Before he turned away, he blessed us;
as if the sign of the cross would multiply the cans and boxes,
said be good, and drove off, down the rutty, muddy lane,
his car scraping bottom the whole way.

Libby Falk Jones

Heritage

I come from a line
of brave women—
My grandmother, Robbie,
sailed to England
on the Queen Elizabeth
at seventy-five, alone
"Did I make friends?
The belle of the ball!"
she put it, many times,
wrinkles be damned,
she danced every night.
Helen, my aunt,
ran with the newsguys
in 1930s Louisiana,
a rare woman reporter
who wrote more than hats
and spinach soufflés,
she covered politics,
hobnobbed with Huey,
unlinked that chain
to the kitchen sink.
And Roberta, my mother,
LSU honors grad
at eighteen, editor
of the '32 *Reveille*,
took on the frat boys,
then traveled dark
New Orleans streets,
social caseworker,
never mind cockroaches
bigger than fists
in that flimsy apartment,
one found her nightgown.
Later, scared of the air,
still she flew
with my father
in a wisp of a plane
over Point Barrow,

they framed the certificate
the pilot signed,
she wheeled
over Bear Tooth Pass
in Montana,
never relaxed,
ignored the abyss,
the auto's thin tires.
Brave to smoke
for fifty years.
Braver to quit
cold turkey,
give up coffee,
take up tea. She
could do most
anything she
wanted to do
and what she
couldn't, she
knew I could.

Libby Falk Jones

The February Morning After We Fight

I oversleep after a rotten wakeful night
asking how can I dedicate my book of poems to you
for your faithful listening
when that's what we were fighting about,

the hour you spent listening
to a silly woman on the phone,
you'd met her flying planes
and now she wanted you
to help her sell her skin care products,
and you couldn't, wouldn't say no—
how could you do that, you lost your whole evening
for writing, I said, *your mother was right,*
I said, *you're too responsible*
and kind for your own good,
it's like phone sex, I said,
it's worse, phone sex wouldn't take an hour—
and you said nothing

and we tried hard all night
not to touch each other

but when I slide bleary-eyed into the kitchen
and say, *have you turned up the heat,*
you say, *come here,*
and you push into my mouth
a quarter of a slice of apple,
fresh as the day we picked it from the tree, you say,

and it is
and you are
and we will.

MARY RUDEN

Centennial 2020, Suffragist Sampler

Rabbit

The orange light of the sun filtered through the curtains. Billy Jean tried to ignore it and force herself back into her dream world, but the day's duties crowded the dreams away. She yawned silently and began carefully sliding her arm out from under her sleeping toddler. She crossed the room to a twin bed and pulled the ragged handmade quilt up under the chin of her sleeping four-year-old son.

In the kitchen she made a pot of coffee and leaned against the sink while the coffeemaker slurped and gulumped a dark stream into the pot. The greasy calendar that hung above the stove, said it was the twelfth of August, her birthday. Today she was legal, twenty-one years old.

As she poured coffee into her cup she heard the springs on the couch groan and her husband, Mickey entered the kitchen from the living room. He stood in the doorway and wiped sleep from his eyes.

"You want a cup?" Billy Jean nodded at the pot.

"No." Mickey shook his head. "I'm gonna get in the bed. Weren't enough room for me when I come in from work last night."

"Lanny's teething, so I let her sleep with me. Don't wake her up," Billy Jean said to Mickey's back as he passed through the bedroom door.

Mickey grunted an answer. Billy Jean felt a little hurt, but how could she expect Mickey to remember her birthday if she'd almost didn't herself. Working nights at the mill kept him so tired he couldn't remember the day of the week, much in less the day of the month.

Billy Jean topped off her cup of coffee and walked out into the back yard. This was her favorite time of day. The birds were singing and the world smelled fresh. The grass was wet and cold on her bare feet as she walked across the yard. She sat her coffee cup on top of the wire chicken run she pulled the lid off a five gallon bucket and threw handfuls of feed to the four hens in the coop.

The hens clucked and fussed as they pecked at the food. "Y'all need to get busy. Only two eggs yesterday. I know it's hot but you got to earn your feed or else." Billy Jean let the threat dangle in the air but the hens ignored it.

Then she moved to the back of the hen house where the rabbit hutch was mounted on the wall. The rabbits scurried to meet her each wanting to get to the feed pan first. With a grunt Billy Jean hefted another five-gallon bucket from the top of the hutch and filled the scoop with rabbit feed. Maneuvering around the ten squirming rabbits she poured the pellets into the feed pan.

The rabbits ignored her and began shouldering against each other to eat. Billie Jean stroked the fur of whichever rabbit moved into her touch. She'd loved the feel of rabbit fur since she was a little girl and her daddy had given her a white and black spotted one for Easter. That was when she could have an animal just to pet on. Billy Jean continued to stroke the soft fur of the rabbits, cupping her fingers around their sides and feeling their fat bellies.

She missed being a kid and getting presents. Maybe her mama would stop by today and bring her something for her birthday. She sure hoped it would be a pair of shoes. She could use them. Her fingers found a haunch that seemed to be fatter than the others.

Quickly, she clamped her hand down and grabbed the rabbit by the back of its neck and pulled it out of the hutch, closing the door behind her. The rabbit kicked and squirmed futilely against her hand, she pulled it in close to her chest, she could feel its heart thumping wildly. "Don't be scared little rabbit." She rubbed her cheek against the white fur. What would it feel like to be covered in something so soft?

Billy jean grasped the rabbit's scruff with her left hand and hefted it a few times. "Yeah, you sure are getting fat." The rabbit struggled against her. Its long back feet searched the air for something solid. It squirmed and twisted until its sharp claws raked across Billy Jean's hand, leaving two red trails. She tightened her grip on the frantic rabbit and watched as bright drops of blood oozed from the twin lines.

"You getting loose wouldn't do either of us any good."

She walked to the far side of the rabbit hutch and stood on a large fat rock. Moving quickly she grasped both of the rabbit's back feet in her right hand. She began to swing it in an arc back and forth. With each arc the rabbit seemed lighter and droplets of blood splashed from Billy Jean's hand onto the rock. Each swing gained speed. The rabbit's struggles slowed and stopped with the movement. It became a weightless, limp, white blur in her hand. When the momentum was right and Billy Jean knew she couldn't get any more force from her swing, whack. She connected the rabbit's skull with the rock. The impact traveled up her arm and left a shudder in her brain.

Billy Jean lay the rabbit's body down on the rock and squatted beside it. The rabbit twitched and a trickle of blood ran out of its big ear and stained the white fur. She watched as death clouded the black eyes. "I'm sorry," she whispered to the dying rabbit. "I don't like killing things and I never wanted to hurt you." A tear slowly ran down Billy Jean's cheek and she angrily brushed it away.

"But it's like this," she said, her voice becoming hard, "my kids wouldn't have anything for breakfast except some biscuits and water gravy." The rabbit stopped twitching and Billy Jean rubbed its fur once again. "That ain't enough for growing babies. They need meat." She pulled the sharp knife from her shorts pocket. "I'm sorry but the good Lord not only give you soft fur, but he made you out of meat." Billy Jean stuck the tip of the knife blade into the soft skin between the rabbit's hind legs and cut through the skin to the breastbone.

Later that morning she watched as her babies smacked their lips and ate tender fried rabbit. She smiled at them and took another bite of her biscuit with water gravy.

LESLIE CLARK

Trajectory

The child learns
to love and be loved,
the magic of words and
how to braid them together,
to delve into books,
to savor the smell of rain
and the taste of tears,
how to sleep
without a night light.

The adult,
awestruck by
the sound of trains,
the voice of an owl,
the red tail feather
a hawk left as talisman,
the whipcrack of thunder,
awaits the inescapable –
the departure of youth,
the ever-changing world,
the ultimate migration
of beautiful lives,
and learns
how to say goodbye.

Leslie Clark

Interior

Drawn-out
summer evenings.
Rind of moon.
Leaves on the
trees are denser,
more privacy
for the birds.

In the maple,
a dusk-red
cardinal twines
in and around.
Quiet, purposeful.

In the spaces
between leaves,
a hint of color
flashes, is gone,
reappears,
pulsing in and out
of the green –
the beating heart
of the living wood.

Ashley Owens

Knots

LACY SNAPP

Heartpine

We repeat words to ingrain them into memory.
Sometimes, the more we say a word, the stranger it feels
on the tongue. Foreign. Like we don't actually know what it means at all.
Juanita. Great-grandmother. I knew her as a child. Well, parts of her. I knew
how she would sweeten her coffee with ice-cream. I knew her jewelry stand
by heart—I'd get on tiptoes to peer into every drawer, marvel
at the broaches, the rings, try with little fingers to clip
Sarah Coventry earrings onto little earlobes. I knew
her everyday necklace, pearls even and
tight like the grain of heart pine.
Heartpine.
When the tree's seed germinates,
for ten years it will only be the height of a blade
of grass. For ten years, its energy is spent strengthening its root system—
most of its universe lies beneath the surface. When it's finally ready, it will grow
an inch wider every thirty years. After her death, I found black and white
photographs of a woman in a pencil skirt and pinned on hat, peeking out
from behind a tree, laughing, whiskey bottle in hand—I learned she slept
with a pearl handle Bauer .25 under her pillow and had five
husbands, some passed of mysterious
circumstances. She voyaged
from Shelton, NC, on a covered wagon with
her many brothers and sisters, dressed in matching
potato sacks, and looking back on the poorness of what was,
wasn't mournful, just wanted more. A pair of shoes for every blouse, tools
of her own, accessories, she'd write her name on anything in Sharpie to claim
it as it came through the door. Every pan in the kitchen. Even the back wall
of her father's cedar armoire.
One Sunday, after her second stroke, Dad loaded us up in the van
to pay her a visit. Measuring tape in his hand, she stood on her tiptoes,
eager for my dad to calculate her height, her width—he told her
that was cheating, she needed to keep her feet flat.
It took us a few months to build her coffin
in the basement.
I was only ten, friends would come over
for sleepovers and be scared of what was in the works
beneath the house's surface. In the end, when her growth rings were getting

closer and closer together, she'd ask
Dad how it was coming along and he'd tell her, to hang on a bit longer,
he wasn't done yet. In a plot with a view at Happy Valley Memorial Park,
she is closer to being reunited with the earth than those encased
in bronze or copper. She sleeps in a bed all her own,
made of reclaimed heartpine.
Heartpine for Juanita.

Lacy Snapp

Us Middle School Nymphs

Brood X cicadas bow down their brown bodies
to tree branches, camouflage behind emerald leaves
for privacy as they lay their eggs. Weeks later

the new born nymphs drop down to the ground,
burrow beneath fresh earth to feast on tree roots'
nectar for the next seventeen years. The last time

they did this was in 2004—as eleven year old me
hid myself amidst swarms of prepubescent girls
in the new middle school hallway, tried to disappear

into acrylic murals painted onto walls of cinderblock:
scenes of Tennessee—the state flag, state flower,
state tree. Timidly, I teetered on letting myself be seen,

only sometimes illuminating as the firefly does—or would
I call myself a lightning bug? I hadn't decided yet.
Meanwhile, boyish raccoon broods wrestled around every

corner. The mockingbirds whispered at the top of the stair.
*These insects appear in these fantastic numbers in every
seventeenth year*, the Swedish naturalist Peter Kalm

noted in 1749 while visiting America. In prior years,
the woods brimmed with a different degree of dusk-silence—
only a lonely cicada or two. Some of Brood X emerged

prematurely in 2017, with whispers of the end of days
close behind. Scientists wondered why the group would divide,
why some were ready to surface years early, climb

the closest vertical object to shed its outer layer and expand wings.
The answer can't be narrowed down to a scientific formula.
Ascending to middle school doesn't mean an immediate

shift for all—I watched as girls my age stuffed push up bras
and began straightening their hair, decorating their faces
all in time for the morning announcements—shedding soft layers

as the tulip poplar does in autumn: golden cardigans draped
over chair backs—daring the teacher to demand them
to re-dress: cover cami tank top straps, thin and brown

as the topmost branches of the tree's canopy.
Some of us chose to stay beneath the ground for longer.
Waiting to emerge shyly as the Iris does, purple petals

unfolding in early May. Or until a warm June's evening
to finally expand hard wing casings, the ones
simultaneously guarding me and holding me back.

I now unveil at twilight: a firefly—I decided.
Not beneath fluorescent bulbs or within walls of stone.
A complex being made of fire and flight.

LACY SNAPP

Red Oak

I.

RIP my childhood red oak.

When you were planted by my father,
you were only the height of a toddler,
but grew to be three stories tall
and would brush your tree-tips across
my bedroom window at midnight,
relentlessly throughout summer storms.

You were the first tree I ever climbed.
It was uncomfortable—I'd hug tight
to your trunk when I needed a rest,
bark would poke through my shirt
into my soft, elementary belly. I felt
ants scurry beneath fingertips but
I was too scared of falling to ungrip.

Fresh-faced stump, you now stare up
at me. In shock. Outraged. Wounded.
Years of shade and afternoon games
dropping sap and acorns on my car
were cut away in a few hours—
a deception that shook every house
on the street, rippled out from the eye
of your rings, confined now to seventeen.

II.

RIP backroad red barn.

You offered wanderers protection as they
braced against the elements in the middle of
a cow field. Unconcerned with the
modern—electricity, fashion—your red
paint flaked proudly until your sagging roof
and old age were no longer charming,

but dangerous. You fought my father with
each rusted nail as he tore you down.

I spread out your seventeen foot limbs,
stick stack sort them, make sure they stay
flat, are prepared to be cut and sanded,
formed into a table or clock, something less
mysterious than an untouched barn at a dirt
road's end. Your worth is now measured by
feet. Inches. How well you can be divided.

I flip your scarlet face away and watch as
silverfish scurry from my fingertips. Hating
the sunlight, but unafraid, when the wood's
movement disturbs them, a new home is
easily found. Soft. Grey. Fluid. Sheltered in
the solid bones of a red oak twice displaced.

Merry Jane

Jonie McIntire

Magnolias and Rosehips

The women in my family don't make friends
so my mother makes wine instead, from rhubarb
to dandelion. In her retirement, she's softened.
She's planted magnolias all over the place.

Rosehip wine this weekend, a simple recipe – the usual
enzymes and yeasts. We do it in late October
because the petals of the roses have fallen
away, just the hard fruit left, protecting seeds.

We are visiting, a grey weekend with teens
about to leave our nest. My mother and I pick rosehips,
wear welding gloves and wander two fence-lines
wearing aprons meant for egg-gathering.

While we trim the stem and blossom bits from the hip,
my mother talks to the kids about our last trip. How
she and I and her sister flew over the Plains, them reading
voraciously and me chatting up every stranger I sat next to.

I catch the barb in the tale — *ingratiating*, that's how
my mother describes it. Describes me.
She grins and shakes her head, says *it helps*
to have a cruise director for a daughter.

We cut and scoop and my mother switches to talking
about the wine. It has to age for two years in the dark,
so we'll have to be patient. She's arguing with herself
about sugar – it calls for 2 and 2/3 pounds

and she wants the alcohol but not the sweet.
Always been like that.
Likes the bitter but hates the sticky.
Like her mother. Like her father.

Her older sister waits to be widowed and has started
calling daily. Still new, this picking past

each other's thorns, still a little tender.
But my mother makes plans to move her here,

later, when she's alone. The magnolias were planted
for her, their spindly stems not yet the sweet explosion
her sister quietly loves. We pour the boiling water over
the bag of chopped rosehips, over the sugar, and wait.

Jonie McIntire

Pittsburgh, 1973

I was born into rolling September hills and smog,
trees sprung up from depression-era jobs
and lines of unemployed waiting outside
rusted steelmills.   Rivers collide and my
Grandmother's voice booms orders
at orderlies and pale-faced nurses. My mother
just wants a smoke and a babydoll
and ends up with a bad first husband
and a colicky infant.   But that happens
later – right now, it's just Grandma
and spinal taps and you can have your
smoke when the girl is out. Nobody's
damn business about the father –
what's in a name? Let me do that –
she doesn't know what she wants.
And my mother closes her eyes and
imagines the sound rolling down the hills,
past the winding streets and
offside driveways, into the valleys
where you could hear a small sound
like a squeal, just above the foundry steam.

JONIE MCINTIRE

Vinegar for Flies

My grandmother recommended sugar
to impress the church-clad lavender ladies,
the neighborhood scout leaders.
Better than vinegar, though as soon as
doors closed she was drywall-shaking
loud, from foot to throat.

My grandfather, oldest son and academic,
didn't need it. He knew how to hold favor —
by directing, by keeping up the good show,
by lining the smart children in front,
the dull in back or not at all.

My grandmother of bad feet and soft biscuits
wanted to go to college to become a nurse,
but my grandfather insisted.
Too many children already,
too much house to care for.
And too stupid, after all.

Even after twenty years of marriage,
I struggle to show love. Instead,
bake pans of brownies late August,
the kitchen a spatter of flour and jars
of apple cider vinegar, fruit flies
trapped under film, struggling to get out.

Tamara M. Baxter

Setting Fire to the Farm

I promised God I'd never strike a match again
if He would *please, please* put out the fire I'd lit
in the dry grass above the barn.
I only wanted to feel the match scratch
the rough brown hem, to see some sparks fly.

I'd like to say, *No harm could come from that.*

The flame took feet, leapt the pasture,
heels sweeping bright from sedge to sedge,
and then, before the fence
the fire stood upright like a man ablaze,
set across the field sowing seeds that sparkled
and sizzled dry blades and left black tracks.
His crackling hands lifted drought-struck branches
that squirmed and screamed before they died---
then quickly, he multiplied into a band of burning men
arm-lashing toward the woods.

The toothless matchbook still in my hand, I prayed.

I'd like to say, *God sent rain.*

Instead, Mama came with buckets of water
and wet towels. We beat back fire for hours—
The barn, the woods were spared,
But not the five calves, burnt-black-winged.
Not the burnt black fields of grain.
Deadfalls still smoking for days, and still no rain.

I'd like to say, *I never struck a match again.*

Tamara M. Baxter

The Moon of Red Cherries

When cherries ripen red,
and the trees laden with fruit,
Grand-Mama Huff sends us to frighten
the black birds from the boughs
----so heavy they weep ground-ward,
    and wobble under the weight of promise----
disturbed now by pesky black bird picking.

The cherry cobblers of winter-making
already baking and bubbling in her imagined
flakey crusts oozing butter are stolen
in the height of summer by thieving birds.

We pick ripe cherries by the dishpan full.
Our tongues pucker eating so many of them.

Since the birds are roosting in the orchard,
we keep picking cherries into night,
our fingers blood-red numbed,
stealing back from the birds our store of winter pies
while the red cherry moon flies east to west
across the bird-struck sky,
and in our grandchild memories,
multiplies and multiplies.

Tamara M. Baxter

Counting Daddy Home

Lying in my bed at night
by the open window
I count Daddy home
out of drunken darkness,
over and over to sixty
measuring moments in my mind
until his junk car rattles
along the road and settles
coughing into the mud-hard ruts.

His car door's screeching hinges
stop the tree frogs screaming
for a second of silence, then,
our old gate swings back and forth
from rusty stupor.

I hear Daddy's plop-plop-plop
of crooked wobbling on the concrete
walk. Mama poured that walk herself
to keep mud out. She mixed and poured
for days, her back hunched over
in hot sun.

At the front porch, Daddy stops
and pees in the pretty-by-nights
Mama planted beside the steps. Mama
is proud of her flowers. She waters
them of evenings, holds their little chins
in her fingers and smiles.

I listen Mama to the door,
strain to hear the heavy hinges
of her condemnation
and his giggling refrain bumping
out of time with my thumping heart,
and wonder what rhythm I can find
to count my Daddy home
out of his black dark night.

AMEE NEAL

Pull Yourself Together

Nancy Posey

Grandma Shares Wisdom, More or Less

Don't look a gift horse in the eye, she warned me
as we ventured together into the livestock show
at the county fair when I, a boy more curious than wise,
stepped too close. She misquoted all the great ones,
Shakespeare, Mark Twain, Jesus Christ Himself.

Neither a borrower nor a blender be, she responded
when I asked her for change, hearing the ice cream man's
music as Grandma sang along—that song about *Casey, who
waltzed with the strawberry blonde and the Band-Aid on*.

Commenting on missteps by well-meaning friends,
she summed up, *When all is said and dumb. . . .*

We learned not to press her for explanation, nor to correct,
accepting that *A stitch in time saves knives*, and *It's better
to give than to believe*. Whether her muse
was Uncle Remus or the Apostle Paul, we nodded
and answered, *Yes, Ma'am*, knowing full well
she had promised she'd never steer us to Rome.

Nancy Posey

Adages

Like fragments of poems, she fed me
wise words gleaned from sages,
passed down from ancestors, never
insisting I listen. She merely sang them,
tunes in harmony with our days, so subtle
I never knew what I had learned, lessons
indelible as tattoos: Haste makes waste;
A penny saved is a penny earned;
A stitch in time saves nine.

Preparing me for a future we'd not share,
she showed me how to thread a needle,
to slide beeswax along the thread,
to tie a knot both sure and invisible.

So now, when missing her, I climb up
on her wooden stool, take down boxes
from the highest closet shelf, unpacking
all her dresses, blouses--broadcloth, wool--
inhale her scent, inspect the French seams,
her tiny, even stitches, hand-tatted lace
trim, the only decoration she allowed
herself. I summon her spirit, her scissors
as sharp as when she wielded them,
laying out fabric she had saved for later,
some special occasion--or perhaps
saved for me. Pressing flat the tissue
pattern, using her silver flatware—
knives and forks instead of pins—
to hold each piece in place, I hear
her voice in my ear, a bit of a melody
whispered, "Measure twice. Cut once."

CJ Farnsworth

Long before I learned Eddie Vedder's head was made into a piñata

And I have to assume it was a Grecian urn gesture and suppress
the natural urge to pummel his papier-mâché face with love
via guitar arms - or is it necks? Wouldn't this be a summer porch-
party game! To bash his crepey head until the surprises inside
spilled out smokey and deep-throated, so deep as to be oceanic,
so deep as to penetrate my ovaries, wherever they are, sweetly,
completely, and fluidly or maybe more gas or plasma-like
- yes, more like those - embedding themselves egg-like

...Jenny and me sat on the porch shakin' grass from our hair
and wasn't that fun too howlin' at the sun on summer days
Daddy on the tractor tearin' up onion grass Mother carryin'
boxes smelled like fruit when I didn't know nothin' 'bout cultural
anthropology or le smoking pantsuits when Jenny's Daddy took us
motorcyclin' 'round WV serpentine turns my chest pressed
like a Seal N Serve thinkin' the whole time about a VW van my one
burnin' eternal 1-2-3 wish then stoppin' by the FarmFresh for candy
bars past Bethlehem School where the honeysuckle swallowed up
the fence and Tyrone sittin' all alone at home with so many ain't cool
cats who some poor fool put bells too tight 'round their necks

Only thing I reckoned then was it's no one but you has to make
your own wreck and ain't that really, though, how we all connect?
So I grabbed up my Steno pad and wrote down:
I'm sending word 'gainst sadness.
Lord, it's summer and sun
don't let these thoughts fade 'way.

CJ Farnsworth

some rare but serious side effects may include

she's thinking in the dark
(dark is for thinking)
about how she hasn't felt a thing
today she'd like to blame the gynecologist

first thing Monday morning:
how was *your* weekend?
(Monday firsts are for thinking things)
 terrible, we found out a(nother) *friend*
has (another terrible) *Lou Gehrig's* (disease),
just spent a lot of time crying the Director of PR&Marketing said
she keeps a tumored dog in diapers
he still seems to enjoy life
she can't bear to put him down

it may have been raining
(rain is for thinking)
when she walked across Main Street to
pay Susan's lunch tab at *The S-Bridge,*
a slab of meatloaf w/o bread and a D.Coke w/ ice
the owner, George D., sat
in a booth cigar smoking,
figuring on green ledger pages

her husband's 34th birthday
cake, w/sweet icing, song sung and a pause
before blowing out the candle-
two wrought iron plant holders w/ fleur de lis designs
Brad Paisley CD - boy from a neighboring town made good-
they're intellectual enough to mock country music
(country music is not for thinking)
but anti-pretense enough
to embrace their cultural heritage

her son climbs into the shower
(showers are for thinking)
she smooths coconut-scented shampoo over
his scalp, he clasps two large, less-than-plastic gems

from a goodie bag his littlebuddy brought back
from Disney World's Pirates of the Caribbean,
the orange one, he explains, doesn't have any special powers
it's just dead, maybe from too much wishing

but she can't explain to a medical doctor
(medical doctors are for thinking)
that shethinks-shewants his little t-shaped plastic stick
removed because she hasn't felt a thing
in a long time,
maybe since he embedded it in her uterus

CJ FARNSWORTH

Endemic Influences on Gamma Rhythms as Noted During the Pandemic

Dinner arrives as I'm thinking about Kurt Cobain
And cigarettes and the way Kurt was a small
Giant

As evidenced by his thrifty professorial cardigan
That I'm sure still smells like cigarettes, though I can't
confirm it

Because the sweater is hermetically sealed in plexiglass
As Holden would want it to be (neither had very involved
Parents)

When the oven buzzes I'm thinking about -ly
Instead, about my ambivalence toward these
Two letters

How I can't go to the bathroom or breathe late
Into a quiet night without fretting about these
Bastards

The same way appropriate parents might fret
About their wayward kid and when I bite into a
Knuckle of chicken

I recognize how cartilage-like, how sinewy, those -ly
sooks are, how I'm drawn to them precisely because
Of their subjugation

Ostracized for their anemic persona, it is their sisters
and brothers who do the cooking and dig the coal
Though families

In my neck of the woods are ambivalent about that kind
of sequestration too and when the melamine plate
Is almost bare

Except for what can't be chewed and what's drained
I lay it atop a book bereft of -ly, a book titled simply
"The Brain"

LEANN COOPER

Dreaming with flowers in her hair

Patsy Kisner

April 2020

I need
a moment
to remember
that the fawns
will soon
be born
and that
the does
will lick
them clean.

ERIN MILLER REID

Save Yourself

Sandra straddled the air. Humidity and the cloying smell of uncured tobacco filled the space between her legs. She balanced on two beams a yard apart and twenty feet off the ground. Every time she bent to grab another rack of tobacco from her cousin on the tier below, the beams groaned, an unnerving Rice Krispies *snap-crackle-pop*. Surely, her uncle wouldn't put her up so high if it was dangerous, or maybe that was why he paid her a little extra on the side.

Sandra needed the money though. In two weeks she'd go to college. Most of her classmates had enrolled in the community college in town, or signed on at the tire plant. A couple of boys had enlisted in the Army, but only a handful of kids were going away to school. She was one of them. Soon there'd be no tobacco barns, no kudzu-wrapped telephone poles, no muddy ponds and chigger flowers, no Sunday dinners with too many creamed vegetables. Though the thought thrilled her, it guilted her too. She should be scheming with P.J., planning a going away party with bootleg beer in an unlit field on the back side of the valley.

Sandra bent and lifted, bent and lifted, tobacco leaves rustling across the rubber soles of her sneakers, then over her jeans and against her dad's work shirt that she wore knotted at the waist. The tips of the leaves grazed across her sweaty cheek as she hooked the stick of speared tobacco overhead. She wiped her face on the cotton sleeve of the borrowed shirt. Three summers ago when she helped top the tobacco in the field, she'd only worn a tank top and cut-offs. It was blistering hot and she'd wanted to work on her tan. She stretched up row after row to pluck flowery crowns from the plants, leaning into the green leaves, sticky like fly paper against her bare skin. By evening, Sandra sat crumpled on the bathroom floor, tanned biscuit brown, her cheek resting on the cool edge of the toilet, retching from tobacco poisoning.

Now, Sandra roasted in the long-sleeved button-up. Her feet were numb, fixed in the same position for hours. She was afraid to move even a toe-length, afraid of losing her balance. At least at the top of the barn there were fewer mosquitoes. Plus, it was quiet. She only heard the rattle of the tobacco leaves, hung like drab, rumpled curtains, and, if she strained, the muffled voices of Waylon and Dolly drifting up from the AM radio.

Sandra could think better when she was high on the crossbeams, and she mostly thought about P.J. Sutton and Richie, and how the summer could've been, could still be, different. She wished life were one of those *Choose Your*

Own Adventure books she'd read as a kid, with do-overs, so she could trial through choices and figure out which was best. Maybe then, she could fix the summer. Maybe then, P.J. could've been saved, and she'd know what to do about Richie.

All summer long he'd been begging her to sleep with him. "C'mon," Richie would say, "You're leaving soon." She couldn't deny that at times sex was all she wanted, especially when Richie slid his hands into the back pockets of her Lee jeans, pulling her close, his warm breath dampening her neck. Just thinking about it made her tingle, like a Zippo lighter flick-flick-flicking between her thighs.

She didn't love him though. He whispered he loved her, mostly when they were tangled up in the backseat of his Chevelle. She'd say, "Love you too," leaving off the *I*. If she waited, she might meet someone at college, someone she adored. Shouldn't her first time be *making love*, and not just *screwing*? Screwing would only make her feel guilty.

But why? Sex was as old as the earth, natural, and pretty much everyone she knew was doing it. Even the kids in her Sunday school class that said they were waiting for marriage had lapsed once or twice. In a basement classroom that smelled like damp carpet, deacons lectured about purity, taking care never to say S-E-X outright. Their teenaged charges stared at a stack of Gideon Bibles in the center of the table, pondering whether their own bodies had already been defiled.

Sandra's cousin hoisted up another rack of tobacco, overloaded and heavy. She heaved it onto the rafter above her. She gritted her teeth as the lip of one sneaker slipped a half-inch on the beam. She repositioned herself, electricity surging from the soles of her feet to her ankles, up her calves, and to her hamstrings.

One night, while doing Trigonometry homework in her bedroom, Sandra overheard her parents downstairs. Her mother clanked around the kitchen, cleaning up after dinner, upset about the preacher's sermon. "He's using guilt to keep folks in line," her mom said. Cabinet doors banged shut. Dishes clattered in the sink. A faucet gushed on, then off. "Quit the church then," Sandra's dad said matter-of-factly. There was a pause. A chair scraped across the floor. Her mom sighed. "I'd feel too guilty." Her parents chuckled, while Sandra scribbled down the tangent of a sixty-degree angle.

Life was too short for guilt, and maybe too short to wait. In the third grade, Sandra won the class spelling bee. The prize was a giant red lollipop, wide as a saucer and studded with rainbow sprinkles. Sandra tucked it away in her nightstand to savor on a special occasion. When she pulled it out a year later, the candy was soft and melted to the cellophane wrapper.

This summer Sandra had waited too long again. Her stomach pitched. Of course, there was no way to know if she'd been anywhere else, if she'd left Richie's house sooner instead of indulging him on his parent's plaid sofa, that P.J. would still be alive.

As kids, she and P.J. met in the church kitchen after the closing prayer to gorge on communion leftovers. They'd huddle over the counter between piles of laundered dishcloths and half-empty jugs of lemonade from the last potluck, and wash down bite-sized wafers with sips of red grape juice, racing to see who could stack the miniature plastic cups the highest. Sandra remembered a particular Sunday when she was twelve, the day she was allowed to wear lip gloss for the first time. It was also the first time she felt that pleasant throb, that premonition of sex. A crumb caught in the sticky sheen on her lips. "You got something on your mouth," P.J. said, brushing it away. His thumb on her lip. A camera bulb flashed in Sandra's belly, casting light up and down her insides, illuminating crevices she'd never noticed before. Maybe P.J. had felt it too.

Sandra squinted, wringing wet from her eyes. Tears or sweat, she couldn't tell. Outside the barn's upper window, she could just glimpse the Sutton property across the field, the white-sided farmhouse at rest, no one running out the back screen door like they'd done as kids, when Sandra and P.J., her cousins and his sisters, had scrambled up these beams, splintered palms outstretched as they balanced across the rafters like tight-rope walkers, never frightened, never considering that one misstep could mean death. Sandra straightened herself, readying for the next tobacco rack. The beams creaked again and Sandra shuddered, imagining her body crumpled on the packed dirt floor below, like a baby bird flipped from the nest, contorted into freakish angles, eyes open, tongue hanging out. Dead too soon and still a virgin.

MANDA NEAL

The Past

Kari Gunter-Seymour

Perfect Pitch

I rode middle school-bound
in the back seat of my aunt's station wagon,
listening to her and mamma sing "Jolene,"
trading verses, harmonizing the chorus,
I'm begging of you please don't take my man!

A few years later it was "9 to 5."
They were fired up and it was Dolly's doing.
This was rural Ohio, the bottom lip
of Northern Appalachia,
right shy of Perry Como country.

The women in my family worked
the TS Trim factory, spitting out
Honda car parts. Started out
on the assembly line, worked their way
up to paint, then detailing, then welding.

The physical labor made their bodies strong,
their future bright and like Dolly,
they weren't taking any shit.
They learned early on about strikes and picket lines,
how important it was to organize.

Brave women in the work force determined
to see their daughters inside college classrooms,
the hell out of factory row.
I didn't know then that I was being raised
by a feminist, taking back her power.

Like Dolly, my mamma would never use that word,
no matter how much she embodied it.
She was proud to hang up her welder's helmet
end of shift, pick up her paycheck, sing in the front seat
of a station wagon with women she loved.

KARI GUNTER-SEYMOUR

Pack Horse Librarians

I mean no disrespect when I say,
during the Great Depression
Eastern Kentucky was a sundered area.
Surrounded by mountains and waterways,
no easy access in or out, nor any proper
education, until the WPA employed
our grandmothers to packsaddle
literacy to the underserved.

This would be the only good thing
coal would do for Kentucky,
coal and the Presbyterians,
donating books and endowment,
twenty-eight dollars a month to any woman
with a horse or mule, and the spunk
to stand up for progress, brave the weather,
backwaters and hollers, to deliver emancipation
by means of bound dissertation.

You need to understand, this was Appalachia,
just before the war to end all wars.
Only women of disrepute were considered
working women by the church.
Christian women labored in the kitchen and fields,
birthed, prayed, died in them, albeit
many Christian women were taught to read,
if for no other reason than the Lord's word
could be used to hold her back.

But this was the New Deal and all bets were off.
Imagine my grandmother, top of her head
barely level with the saddle's front rigging dee,
flaming red hair, a brand of sass all her own.
Packing up at the Pine Mountain Settlement School,
Harlan County, creek beds as roads,
on foot, single file, across crag and clifftop,
sleeping in barns or lean-tos against the cold.
Deliberate as any lineman or mail carrier,
every treatise she carried, a nugget
of gold inside her saddlebags.

Kari Gunter-Seymour

Wash Your Hands Child

It's not a full-on quarantine, but feels like it,
school closings, bars, restaurants, beauty parlors.
I've canceled professional commitments and workshops,
paid gigs I was counting on. I am not alone in my regret.
We are still tempted to enter the land of touching.

I've jammed the cupboards with recommended staples,
scold myself hourly for touching my face,
have washed my hands to the point of crusty
irritation across each knuckle. I know this drill.

My Appalachian grandmother having lived
through the Spanish one herself,
had one rule, about which she was obsessive–
wash up, spit-polish, immediately
upon entering the house.
We could talk with our mouths full,
shove and taunt, build booby traps on the porch,
run amok in the pastures, but before
we set foot inside the house, our shoes were off,
our hands and faces scrubbed,
standing on a step stool in the washroom,
the handpump drawing water fresh from the well.

There was a bar of lye soap,
a soft wire brush and a full inspection
previous to every meal,
a you-know-better-than-that
whap on the backside for any slackers.

She meticulously cleaned
every egg, pork chop, celery stalk,
jars and cans before prying lose their lids,
bleach-scoured counter tops
and porcelain, floors, the bottoms
of our shoes each night.
She always laid a freshly laundered cloth
across the table before dishing up "vittles,"
most of which she had grown and preserved herself.

We gossiped about how our granny was a little off,
constantly complained as we stood in line
for that bristled brush, our bellies
grumbling nearly as loud as our mouths.

Upon her death, we let go of grandmother's ways,
barely taking time to rinse our hands,
our tangibles, stuffing ourselves on-the-go,
processed foods served upsized and sugared,
licking our mucky fingers between bites.

This afternoon my granddaughter,
all seven years of her, fawn-eyed,
tearful, asked me how—
how her tiny hands, unblemished,
perfectly formed, could do me harm.
Hands that have hardly touched this world.
This child and the slow tail-wagging of her dog,
standing exactly six heel-to-toe paces away,
outside my screen door.

SUZETTE BRADSHAW

Food for Thought

My monthly Food Bank box
contains the same again.
Still,
I welcome it.
Even though the peanut butter
reminds me of another of my daughter's
messy diapers,
and the strawberry jam,
the clotted wound
on DJ's head,
where a billystick struck him
for no real reason.
And the rice and macaroni,
maggots in last week's garbage
the city never picked up.
Raisins,
houseflies those
maggots became.
Generic oatmeal,
the color of my grandmother's face,
minutes before her last breath.
Ramen noodles,
tapeworms,
passed by the scrawny gray cat
that showed up on my doorstep.
Like I could give her a better life.

What I really want
is a cold, sweet, watermelon,
wet with sweat.
Thick green skin,
protecting
thicker white rind
protecting
rich red flesh.

I'd raise that thing above my head,
drop it down onto the hot summer sidewalk,

watch it split
open,
then eat only
its seed-free heart.
Leave the rest for crows.

Suzette Bradshaw

Sacrament

The year I turned twelve,
Jesus got in Granny's blood.
That's what killed her.

Every morning at breakfast,
over easy-over eggs
and coarse-ground grits,
she talked to Him, asked his advice.
In the evening as she took supper
she thanked Him
for another day, another meal,
then scraped her plate clean,
so as to show Him how much.

I thought something was up with Granny
when she started forgetting my name,
stopped watching Hee-Haw,
and pitched that nice sheet cake out in the yard
mumbling on about how it tasted like
galvanized roofing tin.
But Mama said it wasn't nothing.
Granny was just getting old
and a little preoccupied with memorizing scripture
hoping to win two prizes in a row from
Preacher Bob's every-other-month
bible-verse contest.

In fact, Preacher Bob was visiting Granny
when she had that first convulsion.
They were reading from the Book of Revelation
and he said it was a sign
the Holy Ghost was rooting in good.
He got so excited he collapsed too
and writhed with her, back and forth
on the cold linoleum shouting
Hallelujah. Hallelujah.

When Mama went next door to check on Granny
a few mornings later,
she found her sitting at the kitchen table
talking out of her head.
Then her eyes rolled back to the whites.
Mama called an ambulance,
then Preacher Bob.

In the hospital they poked her
and tested her and stuck her a zillion times
taking tube after tube of ruby-red blood.
After two days the doctors finally figured out
she had bad lead poisoning.
How in this world?
She didn't drink liquor
home-made or tax-paid.
Didn't eat dirt
like some women craved.
Her house never been painted
inside or out.
How in this world?

Preacher Bob prayed.
The doctors tried a treatment.
Injected her with some kind of chemical
to leach the poison out.
But it wouldn't budge.
On the third night, she died.
Like Preacher Bob said,
the Holy Ghost was rooted in good.

I went with Mama
back to Granny's house
to get a few things for the undertaker
and to help sweep and clean and dust
before the out-of-towners came in.
That's when I found that pretty gold-rimmed plate
painted with a famous portrait of Christ
lying in the kitchen sink.
He stared up at me,
His arms outstretched,

His body all fork-scraped and knife-cut.
His bone-white robe and green-colored wrap faded and
smeared with days-old egg yolk.
It had been first prize in
Preacher Bob's bible-verse contest,
month before last.

I picked it up, turned it over.
Part of His hand rubbed off in mine.
On the back it read:
Come Unto Me and
"For Decorative Use Only."

Suzette Bradshaw

Raindrops

The storm is coming in quickly
the wind whip-snap slapping through oaks and ash,
leaves turning their pale sides upwards in defiance.

Outside in the safe shelter of the porch I wait,
expectant like a Christmas Eve child.

I can hear the rain now,
hustling down the west ridge.
It will make its way to me
as surely as the obligated thunder
speaks for the silent lightening.

I close my eyes, inhale the sharp scent
of raindrops hitting nearby potato hills,
where wombs of black earth nourish and hold a growing brood.

I breathe in the settling smell of ten hundred round drops
mixing with the red clay of my dusty rural road.
Local cars pass with tinted windows rolled up tight.

The first heavy drops fall onto the porch rail,
ricochet wildly onto my hands and face.
On this hot August day
I am anointed by the Alpha and Omega.
In this holy moment I pray that if reincarnation exists,
if I am allowed to come back to this planet again,
I return as a single simple raindrop.

Oh the honor to be one of many that watered the daisy
plucked by the fingers of an adolescent girl,
the flower's petals foretelling
he loves me
he loves me not
he loves me.

How incredible it would be to fall through the freezing sky
change into a tiny speck of sleet
and land with a six sided snowflake
on the outstretched tongue of a laughing child.

Perhaps I could be one of the raindrops
sent down to Texas to soothe the drought-thirsty throat
of a Longhorn cow.

Maybe I would wind up in the pure water of a mountain stream,
help cool the hooves of the big-eyed doe,
as she bounds down the run,
outwits the hungry wolf.

Or the glory…the glory to be the sacrificial drop
that puts out the last hint of fire
from a marching Klan-man's torch.
Oh that I could live yet again,
and leave in this magnificent way,
hissing and having the final say.

Kelly D. Neal

Time

Barbara Sabol

I'm from a one-way bus ticket
—inspired by George Ella Lyon

straight out of that town—factory whistle, iron works,
a dusty smoke stacked skyline. The overheated river's hiss
beneath the Allegheny ridges. Percussion of jake braking
down the mountain's grade.

I'm from rock: granite, limestone, the grainy quarry water
that floated us anywhere else under the blossoming stars.
I'm from watermarks outside the 12th floor of Swanks,
cipher for the city's resilience—rising from two
flooded centuries; citizens still treading water.

I'm from the stone angel who guards the graves
of the unknown drowned at Grand View Cemetery;
from grandparents, never known, who rest there, too.

I'm from compound bow versus five-point buck; hunting season
trumped school. Back pocket Skoal halo. Red neck, blue collar,
pink collar, orange vest, my scratchy Catholic uniform.
Mass every morning. I'm from *O Sacred Head*—

we intoned the crown's piercing meanness, knelt before it
in clouds of frankincense. From the busy confessional—
a tether of venial sins: the cuss, stolen change, the hand
down there. Eve and her serpent; benign Blessed Mother.

I'm from nickel-a-prayer votives and the sanguine back of God
walking away from long unemployment lines—fathers, brothers, sons—
after the mill shut down. Labor unions fisted with dues.
I'm from too-proud-for-welfare, for food stamps.

I'm from green stamps, back yard gardens, sheets on the line,
the ham steak special at the Tick Tock Diner. St Casmir's—
babushkas bent in prayer. From hand-rolled pirogue,
kielbasa reek, cold bottles of Pabst to cap long days.

I'm from the incline plane ascending from factory grind, up
to scrubbed suburbs then down again into the foundry's belly.
I'm from hand-stitched, home-cooked, nothing wasted.
Streetlight curfew, Archie comics, penny candy, four-square.

On frosted mornings the dairy truck's clink announced the frisson
of ice-cold whole milk. From the bakery van still-warm
white bread, Banana Flips; from canned goods stacked
against atomic fall-out. From the nimble illusion of safety.

I'm from Bob Prince's *swing and a miss,* from the hockey puck's slap
across War Memorial ice. JFK and Jesus, framed. I'm from whatever
is not polished, high-faultin', not some Emily's idea of etiquette.

I'm from the sparking trolley that ferried us into town (antique traction token
still in my jewelry box). At home on wheels, I jumped its grooved tracks,
motored past the city's strict boundaries. Their alarm at the threshold;
no backward glance.

I'm from a country of regret, of missing that gritty Shangri-La where
no one left and I returned as guest. Now an exit off the turnpike,
between Lake Erie and the coast. The place a vapor, thick as myrrh,
a recurring dream.

Barbara Sabol

Over-Easy at the All-Night Diner

I dump out the old brew and sizzle up the grill around dawn,
when the third shifters thin out and the day shift rolls in, then
I spot him; red stitching above his breast pocket reads, *Tom.*

In wrinkled coveralls, he leans on the counter and orders eggs
over hard; yolk hard as the August sun (bubbled like fresh tar
under his roller); leaves me his change and downs the dregs.

Most guys take theirs over-easy, they like for the yolk to ooze,
then sop it up with a slice of bread. Most still dreaming, eyes half-
open; maybe wishing the day was already over, but nobody says.

Bet he knocks off same time as me; I follow him home, in my head:
a tidy one-bedroom painted robin-egg blue; pictures on the walls.
We'd sleep in 'til whenever, and then I'd bring his eggs to the bed—

over-easy this time, spread jelly on his toast. Then he turns me once,
easy, over. I notice the color of his eyes. This is where it gets blurry—
we have nothing to say, or say nothing; either way, things get tense.

I'll keep an eye out for a guy with a sewn-on name, to test my theory,
while I sizzle up the grill, scoop out fine-ground jo in no big hurry.

Barbara Sabol

Stella's Dishes

i
Talk of vegetable plots, cures, meager accounts
as mugs clattered from cupboard to oilcloth,
pungent grounds boiling in the pot (hobo coffee
she called it) mixed with the dour odor

of mop water, spent chaw, ham and cabbage
on the back burner. She cradled me against her,
strained coffee into mugs with her free hand.
My grandmother and the aunts clustered

around the large table, mid-day, break. Work-chaffed
hands wrapped this mug—delicate, with a handle
designed for curled index and balancing thumb.
Ceramic no thicker than chipped bone.

Her lips touched my forehead, blew away
steam, then sipped, sighed before she leaned
into the spindled chair back. No painted mouth
ever marred its rim.

ii
Stories replace impossible memories.
On my first birthday she was buried:
52, essential, with another granddaughter
to coddle, a clan to feed, work to finish.

With the urgency of a taproot, I recall
a thick, warm woman with wire-rim glasses,
auburn hair close-cropped, minced smile, sensible
shoes, always an apron tied over her dress.

iii
Three were salvaged decades later
after my grandfather died, the same number
of bodies that had slept per bed
in her house. Some tight sentiment
held them in the cabinet corner,

170

preserved, ready. I recognized them,
asked *can I have them*, knew
what potency they held.
In sway now behind leaded glass
cupboards, custom-finished.
Mornings, I savor Arabica,
fresh ground, drip–brewed, smooth.
More or less unencumbered, I ease
into the day, imagining Stella:
sleeves rolled bicep-high,
with a daily resolve bitter
as her blistered coffee,
drunk black.

Marlene L'Abbe

Metamorphosis

L. RENÉE

Genealogical Trip to Pulaski, Virginia

The mayfly swarm undulates like the perfect hip
roll, mottled bodies plow brown bodies midair.
Wings fade as fine gossamer in June sun
buoyed by a buzz too quick to be caught
by my eye, which doesn't want to bear the witnessing:

how nature persists in getting on with it, publicly —
life, sex, death in the span of a day.
I turn away, overcome by shame. I look through
my Ford's cracked glass at white mile markers blurring
a black highway. Why does our making always begin

in denial? When I find my great-great grandmother,
Frances Houndshell in Census records, branded
mulatto and a mother at age 9, I do not wince. I practice
numbness, focus only on getting back to the alpha mama
who owned her own body, her own name, somewhere

off the coast of Ghana or Nigeria, maybe,
where her breath, not her sweat, was enough
currency. In Virginia, it's common to see the dead
mayflies skip across pavement like flat rocks tossed
sidearmed at a stream's surface, then lodged

in sidewalk cracks, among orphaned pebbles,
sticks and sprigs of grass. I'd rather look
at uncountable rows of tobacco leaves
which leave me breathless, dizzy even. All those
green ears flap like an elephant's hello, hang woody

scents heavy through my car vents like next-of-kin
hugs hugged only at family reunions. In death,
female mayfly lips freeze into an 'O' as if readying
a whistle, as if leaving evidence of 'no,' after the males
give chase, grab their tiny legs, drag them to the ground,

after the mount. It happens like this. Whole lives
purposed for labor and procreation. Night collects

her bounty. By daybreak, bodies pile by the hundreds
on windowsills, in porch corners, in the middle of a passage
pedestrians stroll between a jail and courthouse.

The nice white genealogist at the local library tells me
Frances' age must be wrong, an error in reporting.
But I know a nymph can be snatched from her skin,
molt and molt until she becomes something new,
gains wings, if only for a brief view of the dust

she will soon call home.

L. Renée

Some Nights We Have the Moon

There are no swans here, just corn
        and potatoes pushing past small-
town dirt. I want to be done
        with want, so I tell my feet
to stalk the wheat swaying
        at the edge of a field
past the silos and scythes,
        past the scabbed scaffolding
of the barn's ash skeleton
        where Old Man Blue hung
himself, after rows of turnips
        refused to green. Sometimes
a person can have their fill of loneliness.

Desire is a tick that hides
        on my haunches until
the bite pulses its red
        district light, needling
my already silly goose-
        pimpled flesh, need swelling
like interminable hurricane water.
        When I float inside night's shade
I try not to think of the wreath
        of flies that lined his neck, how
breath left with a tawdry grunt,
        but the stench of death stayed
salty in my mouth and I liked it.

Can blood cover shame?
        The old man wouldn't want his good
church friends to find him
        swaying like that from the rafters,
so I cut the rope, watched
        the body land like some beached star,
five-pointed with arms and legs spread,
        the head bled a halo in perfect circle.
I let the wolf of me spread out
        and howl full-throated at the pearl

in ink clouds, the incessant
            incandescence, my back licked
by air's black thicket.

I shouldn't say what happened next,
            how a thousand centipedes
squirmed beneath my skin, how tufts
            of fur emerged from my pores,
how I bristled like a corn husk crushed
            under a boot. I shouldn't say my teeth
knew exactly what to do with their new
            pointy tips, how top incisors tore
into his flesh as any country
            girl would a waxy plum, careful
not to open the jaw too wide and waste
            the tart juice jolt a tongue longs for.
It is easy to suck clean the marrow.

From any man's flimsy bones, gristle
            ultimately gives, mixes saliva into
a powdery broth, some succor to sweeten
            sorrow's bitter crop. I can't tell you
why the moon reminds me of empty seats,
            the rooms wiped clean of all who
have left us. I can't tell you why I can't let
            my dead rest, why I've always savored
their carcasses. I have never been whole,
            so there was room.

Note: End line taken from Vievee Francis' "A Flight of Swiftlets Made Their Way In."

L. Renée

Fish Fry

Everything delicious is served on Friday.
Jesus should get a do-over for the Last Supper,
since He missed out on the miracle

that is Wonder Bread made paste by perch's
corn-mealed skin sweating Crisco, clinging
like faith to a mouth's roof, even as the tongue

tries to negotiate release, swat freedom for teeth.
We know what delay tastes like.
We have waited for a check that affords us

this feast of fish golden crisp and the glow of black joy.
With Luther Vandross praising us for being bad
on Aunt Mary's 45 spinner, who would call this dinner?

Stove tops bubble with pots of kale and collards
made sides only by smoked ham hock oozing
salty fat, their doneness determined by Mama Joyce

who dips her Too Blessed 2 Be Stressed mug in the pot-
liquor and sips slowly, purses her lush lips and declares:
It got more meldin' to do. Ain't that true for all of us?

She snorts every time Lil' Russell comes by to kiss her highest
cheekbone, his jeans drifting toward hell like he forgot
his real tribe. *Nevermind, no matter, we made it here together*

the Old Timers will say — though they suck their teeth at the sight
of his drawers, at the sight of a Reneger at their Bid Whist table,
at the scent of Dee Dee's too-sweet macaroni and cheese.

We all fall short of perfection like memory, but Uncle Harold
brings us back to where we started: yellow perch biting their ashen
end of a line in Lake Erie's Ohio waters — the place Grandaddy,

wearing his old mining boots, taught generations the patience
needed to stay fed. Uncle Harold will never bring the tartar sauce
Cousin Cathy, out East, developed a taste for. He will fling back his

James Brown-slicked bouffanted crown and howl the sound of hunting
hounds choking on coal dust, remind her she still a West Virginia holler
girl, remind us travels ain't useful without this knowing.

CONTRIBUTOR BIOS:

TAMARA M. BAXTER'S collection of fiction, *Rock Big and Sing Loud,* won the Morehead State's First Author's Award for Fiction, and was published by the Jesse Stuart Foundation Press with introduction by Robert Morgan. Her short fiction, poetry, and essays have been published in journals such as *Artemis, Appalachian Heritage, Wellspring, Mockingbird, Now and Then, Main Street Rag,* and *The Sow's Ear.*

JESSICA WEYER BENTLEY is an author/poet who grew up in the hills of Eastern Kentucky. She is author of the poetry collection, *Crimson Sunshine* and a cowriter for the award-winning series *Grief Diaries.*

SUZETTE BRADSHAW is a self-taught poet, whose work is influenced by daily life, rural memories, dreams, and art. She strives to create poems which cause a bit of heart-flinch and enjoys performing poetry on stage with old-time Appalachian musicians. Her poems have been published in *Dead Mule, Branches,* and more.

KATHLEEN S. BURGESS, senior editor at *Pudding Magazine,* won a 2018 *Sheila-Na-Gig* poetry prize. Recent collections include *What Burden Do Those Trains Bear Away* (Bottom Dog Press, 2018) and *The Wonder Cupboard* (NightBallet Press, 2019). A retired public-school music teacher, she lives in Chillicothe, Ohio. Visit her at kathleensburgess.com

DANIELLE NICOLE BYINGTON is an author and artist living in Johnson City, TN where she teaches composition and literature at East Tennessee State University (ETSU); during early 2020, she also began an educational business, Sight into Insight, which focuses on the relationship of word and image to enhance emotional understanding.

ODANA CHANEY is a sixth-ish generation Appalachian living in West Virginia on land stolen from the Osage, Cherokee, Shawnee, Moneton, Adena and Hopewell peoples. She attended the University of Pittsburgh where she found her voice, but forgot to graduate. Shen writes about dirt, duality, and dearness.

Born in Fairmont, WV, **LESLIE CLARK** has been published in *Pine Mountain Sand & Gravel.* Her poem "To My Cat – Quarantine Day 15," was included in *Postcards from the Pandemic: A Cincinnati Poetry Month 2020* online project. Her chapbook *Driving in the Dark* was published by Finishing Line Press.

After spending over 20 years as a fulltime mom for three children, **LEANN COOPER** returned to her love of drawing and watercolor in the Fall of 2009. She specializes in creating images of flowers, nature and portraits. She's especially fond of combining animals and flowers together. She believes lives are filled with lovely small moments that can easily be missed, therefore it is always her goal to try and capture them on paper. She lives in Knoxville, TN. with her husband and two cats.

Since graduating from BGSU in 2000, **CONNAUGHT CULLEN** has received a MA-Studio from Eastern Michigan University in 2011 and an MFA from Ohio University in 2015. She has participated in several group exhibitions regionally, nationally and internationally. She is currently the Executive Director for Majestic Galleries in Nelsonville, Ohio.

CECILE DIXON is a retired ED nurse who has returned to Appalachia to write and raise goats. Her work has appeared in *Pine Mountain Sand and Gravel*, *Still: The Journal*, *Fried Chicken and Coffee*, *Dead Mule School of Southern Literature*, *KY, Herstory, Voices*, and *Tributaries*. She holds an MFA from Bluegrass Writer's Studio.

JOY DUFFY is an award winning artist specializing in pin-ups, paintings and portraits. She strives to candidly capture each subject. She swims in visual flow that entices the eyes and engages the mind. Her work has been featured in a variety of venues, publications, books and on album covers.

CJ FARNSWORTH has an M.F.A. from the Vermont College of Fine Arts. Her poetry has appeared in *Kenning, Kestrel, Poetry Quarterly, Mountain Scribes*, and *Poetry on the Move*. She is an active member of WVWriters, Inc. She has also written for *WVLiving*. She is a lifelong resident of Wheeling, WV where she currently resides with her husband and son.

DIANA FERGUSON, known in the art community as 'DiFergi,' has shown internationally and is an awarded visual artist. Growing up an army brat and being a latent bloomer, she graduated with a degree in the arts at the age of 40. Her work contains unique stylized images that live in a lively and colorful world. www.difergi.com

SYLVIA FREEMAN, a native of North Carolina, is an artist/photographer, poet and singer. In her mind, all arts overlap and are necessary to her creative spirit. Her photos have been published in Dove Tales, Heron's Nest, NC Literary Review, Fusion Gallery and others. Her award-winning poems are in many collections.

KATHY GUEST is an artist who works with paper as her primary medium. With a BFA in printmaking from Tyler School of Art, Temple University, Philadelphia, PA, she works to make paper pieces as emotive as paintings, using paper faces that are portraits done from life casts. Her website is www.kathyguestpaperworks.com

KARI GUNTER-SEYMOUR'S award-winning poetry collection is titled *A Place So Deep Inside America It Can't Be Seen*. Her work has been featured in numerous publications including *Verse Daily*, *Rattle* and the *LA Times*. She is a poetry workshop instructor, the 2020 Ohio Poet of the Year and Poet Laureate of Ohio.

Pushcart Prize nominee and Ohio native **JENNIFER HAMBRICK** has won numerous awards for her poetry, was selected by former U.S. Poet Laureate, Ted Kooser, to be featured in *American Life in Poetry* and is the frequent recipient of poetry commissions. Hundreds of her poems appear in publication in literary journals.

PAULETTA HANSEL'S seven poetry collections include *Coal Town Photograph* and *Palindrome*, winner of the 2017 Weatherford Award. Cincinnati's first Poet Laureate and managing editor of *Pine Mountain Sand & Gravel*, her writing has been featured in *Rattle, The Writer's Almanac, American Life in Poetry, Verse Daily* and *Poetry Daily*.

JESSICA HELD first moved to Athens from Cincinnati, Ohio, to earn a degree in painting and photography at Ohio University. After graduating and moving around the Midwest, years later she happily settled back in Athens. Home sweet home. Jessica paints functional artwork and teaches youth art camps and art enrichment classes.

MARY ANN HONAKER is the author of *It Will Happen Like This* (YesNo Press, 2015) and *Becoming Persephone* (Third Lung Press, 2019). Mary Ann holds an MFA in creative writing from Lesley University. She currently lives in Beaver, West Virginia.

LIBBY FALK JONES' poems and creative nonfiction have been published regionally and nationally. Her poetry chapbook, *Above the Eastern Treetops, Blue*, appeared in 2010 (Finishing Line Press). A co-authored collection, *Balance of Five*, came out in 2015. A past president of Kentucky State Poetry Society, Jones is Professor Emerita of English at Berea College, Berea, KY.

STEPHANIE KENDRICK is an Ohio poet. She works for Athens County Board of Developmental Disabilities and Albany Village Council. A co-founder of RoseElaine Productions, she produces a bi-monthly Open Mic and submission workshop. Her work has been published in *SheilaNaGig, Ghost City Review, Northern Appalachia Review, Backdrop Magazine* and others.

PATSY KISNER'S poems have appeared in journals such as *Pine Mountain Sand & Gravel, Appalachian Journal*, and *Sheila-Na-Gig*. She is the author of two poetry collections, *Inside the Horse's Eye* and *Last Days of an Old Dog*, both from Finishing Line Press.

MARLENE L'ABBÉ is inspired by her experiences of life and the world of nature. She studied art in Montreal, Quebec and currently lives in Athens, Ohio. She exhibits her paintings locally, and her art tiles under the name Waterspider Designs which are available at a variety of shops in Athens, Ohio.

KAREN SALYER MCELMURRAY is the author of *Wanting Radiance,* a novel, released in April 2020 from University Press of Kentucky. She is also the author of *Surrendered Child: A Birth Mother's Journey,* a memoir. Her essays have been awarded the Annie Dillard Prize and the Orison Anthology Award.

Jonie McIntire, poet and community builder in Toledo, Ohio, has authored chapbooks *Beyond the Sidewalk* (Nightballet Press, 2017), *Not All Who Are Lost Wander* (Finishing Line Press, 2016), and *Semidomesticated* (which is expected to print later this year.) Jonie hosts monthly readings and workshops. Learn more about her at https://www.joniemcintire.net.

Wendy McVicker is a longtime Woman of Appalachia participant, Ohio Arts Council teaching artist, and current poet laureate of Athens, OH; author of *The Dancer's Notes, Sanctuary,* and *Sliced Dark,* an art/poetry collaboration with John McVicker. She often performs with musician Emily Prince, as the duo *another language altogether.*

Mimi Railey Merritt spent the '80s as a newspaper reporter before a brief stint writing computer manuals, followed by 25 years as a communications professor at Bluefield College. She lives in Bluefield, WV, and now writes poetry and essays and anything else she is not required to.

Sara Minges is an International Speaker and Poet, Best Poet of Kansas City Award Nominee (2019-2020), University of Tennessee-Knoxville alum, Founder of Wonder Woman Rising and former panelist for Lady Gaga's Foundation. Her third full length collection, *Whiskey Sweet,* is forthcoming in Spring 2021 from Black Heart Press.

Barbara Marie Minney writes personal and emotional poetry that describes her feelings, thoughts, and passions while struggling to live her truth as a transgender woman. She began her transition to living authentically as the woman that she now knows she was meant to be at the age of 63 after repressing her true gender identity for over 60 years.

Amee S. Neal lives in Apple Grove, West Virginia where she spends her time cake decorating, writing stories, creating fan art and exhibiting her work. Amee currently has children's book illustrations published. She is one of four siblings who all share a love for art.

Kelly D. Neal is from Apple Grove, West Virginia and the mother of four artistic daughters: Emalea, Amee, Amanda and Kelle. She considers them her greatest works. Neal enjoys writing poetry (with several poems published) and the occasional art project. She hopes to someday publish an illustrated collection of poetry.

Manda Neal grew up on a farm in Apple Grove, West Virginia with her three sisters. Neal has her BFA in Theatre Performance and a minor in Dance from Marshall University. She is currently obtaining her MFA in Acting at Ohio University in Athens, Ohio and will graduate May 2021.

Karen Whittington Nelson lives in rural Southeast Ohio. She attended Ohio University and had careers in both nursing and teaching. Her most recent short story can be found in the *Anthology of Appalachian Writers, Volume XII*. Her poetry and prose appear in the *Women Speak Anthologies*, *Gyroscope Review* and *Pudding Magazine*.

SUSANNA NESTOR moved from Southeast Ohio to Taos, New Mexico in 1977 after pursuing degrees from Ohio State University and Cleveland Marshall Law school. She pursued agribusiness before retiring with lots of horses and grandchildren on her high mountain ranch. She recently completed a Hindman Settlement School Makery fellowship.

CORIE NEUMAYER, a painter in Louisville, Kentucky, works mainly in acrylic, latex, found papers, and aerosol. Her formative years were spent in the rural areas of Rowan County Kentucky which continues to influence her work. Her paintings are in public and private collections, and she has shown regionally and nationally.

VALERIE NIEMAN'S most recent books are *To the Bones*, a horror/mystery set in the West Virginia coalfields (2019), and *Leopard Lady: A Life in Verse* (2018) which was featured in WOAP last year. She is a graduate of West Virginia University and Queens University of Charlotte and teaches writing at NC A&T State University.

HOLLY NORTON is a professor at the University of Northwestern Ohio. She teaches English composition and electives such as Myth and Fairy Tales, Gothic Literature, and Women Who Rock. Her chapbook, *Letting Go*, was published in 2017. Her poems have also been published in *Poets to Come* and *Women Speak*.

ASHLEY PARKER OWENS is an Appalachian writer, poet, and artist living in Richmond, Kentucky. She has an MFA in Creative Writing from Eastern Kentucky University and an MFA in Visual Arts from Rutgers University.

V.E. PARFITT grew up in northern Appalachia and the pull of the hills and hollows is strong, but the pull cannot overcome the sheer economic reality of the area. Funny how even the not-so-good memories and the hardships can seem lit from within when the light hits from a just-so slant. She writes when the sun slants in just that way. She currently makes her home in northeastern Pennsylvania.

TINA PARKER is the author of three books of poetry—*Lock Her Up, Mother May I*, and *Another Offering*. She grew up in Bristol, VA, and now lives in Berea, KY.

LINDA PARSONS is the poetry editor for Madville Publishing and reviews editor for *Pine Mountain Sand & Gravel*. She coordinates WordStream, WDVX-FM's weekly reading/performance series, with Stellasue Lee, and is copy editor for *Chapter 16*, the literary website of Humanities Tennessee. Widely published, her fifth poetry collection is *Candescent* (Iris Press, 2019).

A native of Alabama, **NANCY POSEY,** lived more than twenty years in Western North Carolina with a window view of Grandfather Mountain and Table Rock. Now living midway between in Tennessee, she spends time teaching, reading, writing, and enjoying family and music.

SUSAN E. POWERS holds a BFA from Carnegie Mellon University with a minor in Creative Writing, and an MFA in Painting from Pratt Institute. She is an Adjunct Lecturer in the Art Department of Carlow University in Pittsburgh, PA. Her writing is influenced by immigration and labor history, memory and the sentient natural environment.

VICKI PRITCHARD has been a nurse in Appalachian Ohio for fifty-five years. She has seen first- hand and relied upon, the forgotten bedside work force of essential care-givers who labor for minimum wages.

BONNIE PROUDFOOT lives in Athens, Ohio. Her poetry recently appeared in *Pine Mountain Sand & Gravel* and *Sheila-Na-Gig*. Her story, "Old Spirits" placed first in the 2020 *Sand Hills Journal* national competition. A first novel, *Goshen Road,* set in West Virginia, was published by Swallow Press in January, 2020.

ERIN MILLER REID is originally from southeastern Kentucky and now works as a dermatologist in Kingsport, Tennessee. She has had fiction and poetry published in *Still: The Journal*.

L. RENÉE is a third-year MFA candidate at Indiana University, where she has served as Nonfiction Editor of the *Indiana Review*. Her poems have been published or are forthcoming in *Tin House Online, Poet Lore, the minnesota review, Southern Humanities Review, Appalachian Heritage* and *New Limestone Review.*

McKENNA REVEL grew up in Mount Sterling, Kentucky, called "the gateway to the mountains." She now lives in Lexington, Kentucky. She has been published with *The Girl God*. This will be her second year participating in the Women of Appalachia Project.

MARY RUDEN taught college level art for over eight years. Her artwork and sculpture has been featured in public art projects in several states. She was awarded a Preservation Award by the Knox Heritage East Tennessee Preservation Alliance. Her bronze statues and recent quilts feature historic people. See maryruden.com.

From Apple Grove, West Virginia, **EMALEA NEAL RUPE** earned her Associate Degree in 2013 and BFA in Visual Art from the University of Rio Grande in 2016. Rupe has exhibited in various shows and murals in Rio Grande, Ohio. She accepts many different art projects as well as drawing/painting commission portraits.

Barbara Sabol's second full-length book, *Imagine a Town*, was awarded the 2019 *Sheila-Na-Gig Edition*'s poetry manuscript prize. Her poetry has appeared widely in journals and anthologies. Barbara's awards include an Individual Excellence Award from the Ohio Arts Council. She lives in Akron, OH with her husband and wonder dogs.

Portraits are but one of the numerous collections by artist **Tere Sager**, and portraits of fellow proud Appalachians are particularly dear to her heart. She concentrates mainly, but not solely, on watercolour and encaustic. She currently exhibits her art at Starbrick Gallery in historic downtown Nelsonville Ohio.

S. Renay Sanders learned to love the spoken word amidst a family of storytellers, secretly writing her own stories as poems. She is venturing into storytelling based on her memories and family tales. Her poetry can be found in her chapbook *Dancing in Place* and various anthologies.

Susan Truxell Sauter's poems appear in *Apalachee Review, Anthology of Appalachian Writers, WOAP: Women Speak, Vol. 3, 5 & 10th Anniversary Collection, Nasty Women & Bad Hombres, Fracture: Essays, Poems, & Stories on Fracking in America*, and many volumes of *Voices from the Attic*. She lives in West Virginia.

Karen Scott is a poet and substitute teacher in Columbus, Ohio. A member of Ohio Poetry Association (OPA), a past participant in the Women of Appalachia Project, and a proud member of the SALON writing group. Some of her work has been published in various anthologies.

Marcia Shubert's early interest in photography can be tied to a close ancestor, Percy Loomis Sperr. Sperr was the official New York City photographer during the 1920–40's, and her grandmother, Julia Loomis Staniland, bought her first camera. She attended Ryerson Polytechnical Institute in Toronto, Canada. She considers this medium a vital and important part of her life.

Rose M. Smith's work has appeared in several journals and anthologies. She is author of four chapbooks, most recently *Holes in My Teeth* (Kattywompus Press, 2016). Her collection, *Unearthing Ida* (Glass Lyre Press, 2019), won the 2018 Lyrebird Prize. She's an Editor with Pudding Magazine and a Cave Canem fellow.

Anna Egan Smucker is the author of nine books including *No Star Nights* (Knopf). A resident of Bridgeport, WV, her poems have been published in anthologies and literary journals. Her first poetry book, *Rowing Home*, was published by Finishing Line Press in 2019. She lives in Bridgeport, WV. www.annasmucker.com

Lacy Snapp lives in Johnson City, Tennessee and works as both an adjunct professor of Literature at ETSU and a carpenter, running her self-owned business: Luna's

Woodcraft. She is a board member of the Johnson City Poets Collective and has been published in *The Mockingbird*.

A lifetime lived in Southeastern Ohio informs everything **LOIS SPENCER** writes, most particularly her memoir, *In the Language of My Country*, and recent stories published in *Women Speak* and *Anthology of Appalachian Writers*. Borrowing Grace Paley's words, Lois believes her purpose as a writer is "to tell the truth in the language of the country [I'm] in."

KATHARINE STUDER traced her grandparents seven generations back, discovering they lived in Carter County and Elliott County, Kentucky for hundreds of years. Even though her father moved the family to northern Ohio to work at a factory that would pay a decent living wage, her ties to the hills of Appalachia are her true identity.

BETH JANE TOREN hopes to develop her knowledge and increase her value by flatlander standards. She extracted herself for higher education, exploited herself to pay for it. Home again, she is not buying or selling. She is staying to nurture the people and land in what remains of her mountain home.

PAGE TURNER is an assemblage artist who collects items of deep personal meaning to create delicate sculptural pieces infused with a new feminist aesthetic and a soulful reverence for her Mormon Feminist heritage. Recently featured in *50 Contemporary Women Artists: Groundbreaking Contemporary Art from 1960 to Now,* her work is grounded in the Appalachian region of Virginia.

KELSIE TYSON is an Appalachian multimedia artist. Her artwork is heavily focused on Fat Liberation within Appalachia and how it intersects with Black and Queer Liberation.

KRISTI STEPHENS WALKER is a writer and editor whose work has appeared in various print and online publications. A native of Charleston, West Virginia, she often writes character and setting that reflect the uniqueness of life in her hometown. She currently lives in Nashville, TN with her husband and three children, where she recently completed her first novel.

KRISTINE WILLIAMS lives and writes in Athens, OH. Her chapbook, *Like an Empty House* (Finishing Line Press), comes out in January, 2021. She is retired from teaching communication courses at a local technical college. She lives with her husband and has two adult children who credit her with a love of both writing and teaching.

BIANCA X, Ph.D., is an award-winning writer and multidisciplinary artist from Kentucky. An Assistant Professor of English at Ohio University, Bianca is the author of five collections of poems, most recently *Black Mermaid* (Argus House Press, 2018), and the co-editor of three poetry anthologies, most recently *Black Bone: 25 Years of the Affrilachian Poets* (University of Kentucky Press, 2018).

Katherine Ziff lives in Athens, Ohio, having arrived with her family 22 years ago from the eastern edge of the southern Appalachians. She is retired from counseling practice and now makes flower essences and art. She is the author of *Asylum on the Hill: History of a Healing Landscape*.

Sheila-Na-Gig Editions